WHACKED

THE LUCIE RIZZO MYSTERY SERIES

ADRIENNE GIORDANO

THE LUCIE RIZZO MYSTERY SERIES

Dog Collar Crime

Knocked Off

Limbo (novella)

Boosted

Whacked

Cooked

Romantic suspense books available by Adrienne Giordano

PRIVATE PROTECTOR SERIES

Risking Trust

Man Law

A Just Deception

Negotiating Point

Relentless Pursuit

Opposing Forces

HARLEQUIN INTRIGUES

The Prosecutor

The Defender

The Marshal

The Detective

The Rebel

JUSTIFIABLE CAUSE SERIES

The Chase

The Evasion

The Capture

CASINO FORTUNA SERIES

Deadly Odds

JUSTICE SERIES w/MISTY EVANS

Stealing Justice

Cheating Justice

Holiday Justice

Exposing Justice

Undercover Justice

Protecting Justice

Missing Justice

STEELE RIDGE SERIES w/KELSEY BROWNING

& TRACEY DEVLYN

Steele Ridge: The Beginning

Going Hard (Kelsey Browning)

Living Fast (Adrienne Giordano)

Loving Deep (Tracey Devlyn)

Breaking Free (Adrienne Giordano)

Roaming Wild (Tracey Devlyn)

Stripping Bare (Kelsey Browning)

Whacked: A Lucie Rizzo Mystery
Copyright © 2017 by Adrienne Giordano
(Original title Dog Collar Chaos)
ISBN: 978-1-942504-20-7
Cover Art by Lewellen Designs
Editing by Gina Bernal

All rights reserved. No portion of this book may be used or reproduced in any manner without the express written consent of the author, except in brief quotations embedded in critical articles and reviews.

This is a work of fiction. Names, characters, places, and incidents either are the product of the author's imagination or are used fictitiously, and any resemblance to actual persons, living or dead, business establishments, events or locales is entirely coincidental.

WHACKED

A Lucie Rizzo Mystery
by
Adrienne Giordano

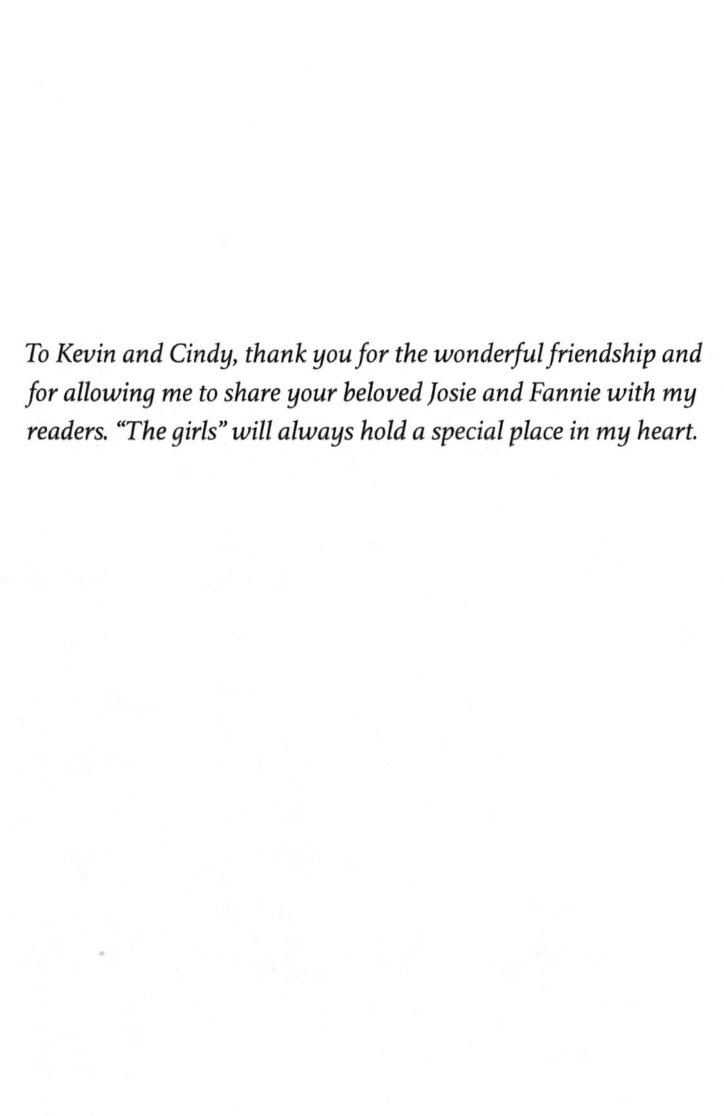

To Kevin and Cindy, thank you for the wonderful friendship and for allowing me to share your beloved Josie and Fannie with my readers. "The girls" will always hold a special place in my heart.

1

———

Some animals were just not built for bathing suit modeling.

Lucie watched her favorite client, an Olde English Bulldogge named Otis, lumber down the runway toward her. His big body moved with the speed of a snail, while the attractive blonde holding his leash did a slow-mo version of the strut only experienced models could pull off.

Otis stopped to lick his parts, the ones squeezed into a too-tight swimsuit, and the blonde looked over at Lucie, her pretty face twisting into a mass of panic and confusion.

"What should I do? He just *stopped*. What happens if he does that in the actual show? This dog could ruin my career."

"Luce," Ro said, "I know you love Otis, but those fitted swim trunks aren't working for him. He's too fat. And, hello, she's right. Is he going to stop and lick his privates in the middle of the show?"

Lucie sighed. Already two hours into this ordeal, she sat on a director's chair in the middle of a hotel ballroom for the latest round of doggie auditions. They'd been at it since eight a.m., and Lucie's mid-morning sugar craving kicked in. Or maybe she simply needed chocolate to get her through this nightmare.

Beside her, Roseanne, Lucie's BFF and Coco Barknell's vice president of sales, furiously jotted notes about each of the prospective models. Stubby legs. Long neck. Big head—all of it on paper for future deliberations. Deliberations that would surely force Lucie to poke her eyes out.

With a screwdriver.

Who knew finding canine models for a charity fashion show could be so difficult?

"He's not fat," she said. "He needs a bigger size."

Ro pointed one well-manicured finger. "That's the XXL."

"Your designs run small."

Ro laughed. Of course she did. They both knew Ro's designs didn't run small. Otis was simply a big boy.

Day four of auditions wasn't going so hot. The biggest issue was fitting the dogs for Ro's unforgiving designs. An extra pound here or there would throw the whole ensemble off.

Fifteen doggie outfits needed models. They'd already gotten lucky and managed to fit two dogs with multiple outfits—thank God for V-necks and belts. But they were still short six dogs.

A yip, followed by an "ouch" came from behind a rolling screen that doubled as a curtain. A round of barking and growls followed, and Lucie clawed her fingers into her scalp.

"Is everything all right?" she called.

"Ow." A hand appeared from the side of the screen. "Fine. We're fine. Ow! This little one is an ankle biter. Shit. Ooh, sorry."

The screen fell over and five dogs leaped on top of it, two of them tugging free from the models holding their leashes.

"Here we go," Ro said. "Ladies, you need to hold those leashes."

The two dogs shot by Lucie and Ro, and Lucie swiveled around to track them. A few volunteers stood behind them waiting for assignments. One of them sidestepped, blocking the dogs' path. Both animals skidded to a stop. Just like that, bam. A spurt of jealousy rose inside Lucie. One day, she'd have that obvious command over these animals. Now? Not so much. When they saw Lucie, they saw fun and playtime and love.

Not a pack leader.

"Wow," Lucie said. "She's good."

"Sure is. We should hire her."

The volunteer walked the dogs back to the once-again-erect screen, and handed the leashes off.

Buzzy Sneider, Lucie and Ro's much more famous partner in this charity gig, and her assistant slipped into the ballroom via a side entrance. The pet product mogul had more damned assistants than the president, but Reece seemed to be the most senior of the bunch.

Please don't let Ro see them.

"Ooh," Ro said, "there's Buzzy. We need to talk to her."

Thanks, universe, for the help. "Uh, no we don't. You promised to let me handle it."

"And I have."

Ha. Good one.

Buzzy's claim to fame came from designing custom dog houses for celebrities and the filthy rich. In the animal world, she carried a lot of weight. If she endorsed a product, it immediately broke sales records.

The problem was, Buzzy had decided to expand her empire to dog accessories and clothing, acting as if she'd created the industry Lucie and Ro had been operating in for nearly a year.

In short, Ro wasn't happy about Buzzy's expansion. Neither was Lucie, but, as the levelheaded half of the dynamic duo, she'd taken the high road and approached Buzzy to partner with Coco Barknell for the fashion show.

Buzzy's mass appeal could only help spread the word about an exceptional non-profit that provided service dogs to people in need. And, oh, right, Coco Barknell.

A win-win.

Except...

Ro maneuvered out of her chair and straightened her blouse. "I don't care what that bitch says, she stole my design. Staff error, my butt. I worked on that leather bomber for months. I knew it would be a hit, which is the only reason I even wanted it in the fashion show."

"*Stole* is such a nasty word."

"But a fitting one."

Lucie peered beyond Ro, where Buzzy stood reviewing a clipboard while her assistant waited for the queen to rule. Poor Reece. In every meeting, the girl had been given a list of tasks that would take a team of twelve to complete. Buzzy, in her infinite wisdom, obviously had no issues nearly killing her staff with work. Still, Reece handled it all with grace and a steadfast attitude that Lucie admired.

Dark hair whirled and the click of spiked heels sounded as Ro headed for Buzzy.

"Ro!" Lucie hopped off the director's chair, narrowly avoiding a faceplant.

Sometimes it sucked being the petite one. At least she'd opted for jeans and sneakers—as opposed to Ro's tight black skirt and stilettos—and easily caught up. Using enough force to get the *keep-your-trap-shut* point across, Lucie latched onto Ro's elbow. "Let me handle this."

One thing they didn't need, no matter how righteous, was Ro beating the crap out of a television queen.

Drama, drama, drama. All because, two days after Lucie and Buzzy signed the fashion show contract, one of Ro's designs turned up for sale on Buzzy's website.

A mistake, Buzzy claimed. A simple oversight by her staff.

"Hellooo," Ro called to Buzzy. "Good morning!"

Disregarding Reece, Buzzy offered a smile that packed a whole lot of prowling lioness behind it. Still, her pixie cut blonde hair and sparkly blue eyes gave her a look of innocence that Lucie found off-putting for a mogul.

"Ladies," Buzzy said, "good morning. How are auditions going?"

Lucie elbowed around Ro, bumping her and knocking her sideways. *That'll teach her for wearing stilettos.* "I've got this," she muttered. "Auditions are great."

Another round of yips and barks and ouches sounded, and the screen—once again—

fell over, landing with a smack that echoed and strained Lucie's last millimeter of patience. She angled back to where two of the shelter dogs rolled over each other, offering up play bows on top of the screen.

If they weren't so darned cute...

"This dog is a jerk," one of the models shrieked. "I'm out of here."

Lucie winced. "Couple of hiccups with the dogs. Nothing we can't handle."

"I'm sure," Buzzy said.

Ro recovered from her teetering and lifted her chin.

"Buzzy, where are we on that design issue? I see it's already on backorder, which means—"

"People love it," Lucie blurted.

"Um." Reece slid the clipboard from Buzzy's grasp. "I'll go check on the dogs. See if I can settle them down."

Buzzy waved her off. "Of course they love it. It's fabulous."

"And *not* yours," Ro said.

Yikes-a-roo. So much for Lucie handling it.

Lucie cleared her throat. "Any word on how this horrible mistake happened? More importantly, how we *fix* it?"

Human error, Lucie understood. But in a company the size of Foo-Foo Entertainment, each product went through several reviews and approvals before being put on sale. And Lucie, as forgiving as she liked to consider herself, wasn't buying human error at every interval.

Still, in an effort to salvage some sort of working relationship—and get through the fashion show—Lucie had given Buzzy a week to get it sorted out.

Buzzy slid her gaze from Lucie to Ro and back. "I'm sorry it's taking so long, Lucie. But you did say a week. We still have one day to investigate."

Now Ro stepped forward, a determined fire sparking in her coffee-brown eyes. Between her long legs, curves, blazing sense of style and a face fit for the cover of Vogue, Ro tended to command space.

Sometimes, it was scary as hell.

Like now.

"The fact that you're making a bazillion dollars on the sales wouldn't be slowing down your investigation, would it?"

Buzzy met Ro's stare and clucked her tongue. The sudden urge to pee assailed Lucie. Damned flop peeing.

"Okay," Reece said from behind her. "Let's get this chubby dog out of here and separate those two. They're troublemakers. Did he just whiz on you? We need a mop! Stat. The urine will burn right through this wood."

Knowing Reece would handle the dogs, Lucie focused on the issue unfolding in front of her. She slid in front of Ro and held up her hands. "Ladies, we're all business people here. Let's stay calm."

"Oh, I'm calm," Ro said. "Do the right thing, Buzzy, and compensate us for the design you stole."

"What's going on?"

Lucie swung around. Buzzy's older sister, Lorraine, stood a foot away, listening to the exchange. Lorraine tucked her shoulder-length hair behind her ears, exposing a heart-shaped face so similar to Buzzy's they could have been twins. Though she'd attended each of the fashion show meetings, Lucie hadn't quite determined Lorraine's role at Foo-Foo Entertainment. "Nothing," Buzzy said. "We're discussing the design that someone mistakenly put up on our website."

Ro snorted and Lucie glared at her. The mean face.

"Oh." Lorraine said. "That."

She locked eyes with Ro and the tension level shot up with enough force to blow a hole in the ceiling.

Lorraine may have been the bigger of the two sisters, but challenging Ro wasn't the brightest of ideas. Clearly, Lorraine hadn't seen what Ro did to Tiffy Nelson in the third grade. That had been the last day Lucie was teased by bullies.

All thanks to Ro.

This time? She couldn't let Ro do the dirty work. This was business.

"Yes," Lucie said. "*That*. It's a nasty little loose end we should tie up. One I feel confident Buzzy will make right by tomorrow."

Lorraine exchanged a look with Buzzy. One of those older sibling, *you-did-it-this-time* looks Lucie knew well. Only, in Lucie's case, it worked in reverse since she tended to be the one pinning her idiot older brother with it.

"I'm sure that won't be a problem." Lorraine angled her head at Buzzy. "Right?"

"Of course. I said a week and it'll be a week."

Ro smacked her hands together. "Excellent. I'd really hate for this to get ugly. And, trust me, it'll get ugly."

"That bitch."

Two hours after the failed auditions, Lucie sat at her desk checking the formulas in Coco Barknell's latest P&L while Roseanne fumed from across the room.

Drama with Ro was nothing new. Just another day in the life of a high-strung diva, but Lucie needed to get this spreadsheet over to the accountant. Ro on a tear would eat up precious time.

"Which bitch are we referring to?"

Ro looked over the rim of her snazzy reading glasses. "Hardy-har. You won't be cracking wise when I show you this."

Oh, the drama.

"Okay, I'll bite. What is it?"

"Buzzy Sneider!"

Lord. Not again.

"What now?"

"She stole another one of my designs!"

Here we go again. "I doubt that."

"I can prove it."

Ro hopped up from her desk, made her way across the aisle separating their workspaces, and shoved her cell phone in Lucie's face.

"Exhibit one. The chinchilla vest."

Sighing, Lucie snagged the phone and studied the photo. The vest *did* appear similar to one Ro had presented to Buzzy as an option for the fashion show.

Concerning? Yes. Particularly after the most recent mix-up with a Coco Barknell design. But an online ad wasn't exactly solid proof. "There are plenty of chinchilla vests out there."

"Dream on. See the buttons? They're rhinestone. Just like mine. At first, I thought the faux fur mixed with rhinestones was over the top, but then I saw it on those crazy Ninja Bitches and figured, eh, kinda cute. And now! Now this bitch stole my design. Again! I should wrap my hands around that scrawny neck of hers."

Huhn. Lucie zoomed in on the rhinestone buttons. *Darn it.* "Where did you find this photo?"

"It's the bitch's website. *Again!* Right there on the homepage." She smacked her hands against Lucie's desk. "I'm so mad right now."

"I see that."

"That damned Buzzy."

Ro spun away and paced in front of Lucie's desk, her skirt straining against the swing of her continually expanding rear. Another thing Lucie heard the railings about day in and day out. Somehow it was Lucie's mother's fault that Ro had gained weight. According to Ro, too many dinners at the Rizzo house equaled a giant ass.

"You weighed yourself again, didn't you? I keep telling

you to stop. Once a week is plenty. Every two hours? Not so much."

"I can't help it. Do you know how much weight I've gained since I started dating your brother?"

"Twelve point five pounds."

"Twelve point five pounds!"

Lucie gave her a winning smile and Ro waved her fists. "Argh! You don't understand."

True that. How could she? Lucie was one of those people cursed by her metabolism. While most struggled to take weight off, she struggled to keep it on. Her body simply worked in reverse. The more she ate, the more her system burned. Add her giant boobs to the package and nothing fit right. She had the lower half of a seven-year-old and the upper half of a Playboy model. Go figure.

"You're right," Lucie said, "I don't understand. I dream of being built like you. I'm built like a fire hydrant. All my weight at the top, if you know what I mean."

"It's the stress," Ro said, still pacing. "And your mother's cooking. The only positive about Joey and I fighting is that I haven't been to your mother's in three days. I should have lost six pounds by now—and don't even comment on the ice cream."

Lucie laughed. The day before, she'd found three pints of ice cream in the break room freezer. Ro told her not to touch them because she was planning a three-way with Ben & Jerry.

Again, Lucie held up her hands. "I'm not saying anything."

"Good. Because I don't need any more aggravation. How many designs does she have to swipe before you get upset?"

Oh, she was upset. Yes, sir. But being the daughter of Joe

Rizzo, mafia boss, had conditioned Lucie to a life filled with disappointments. Her pain tolerance ran higher than most.

When Lucie went to war, she did it by using her brain. And the legal system.

"Screaming about it won't help. After Buzzy started selling the leather bomber, I called our lawyer to see what our options might be."

"You did?"

"I did. I'm not going to let someone do that to you. Unfortunately, the lawyer doesn't think we have sufficient evidence to prove Buzzy stole the design. Which is why I gave her the week to make it right." She handed the phone back to Ro. "Are you scanning your sketches every day like I asked?"

"Yes." She pointed over her shoulder at the rolling garment rack that held the latest samples of her designs. "And I'm taking pictures of everything. Just in case."

"Good. If she's stolen another one, we'll have a dated digital file as proof."

For insurance, Lucie had started backing all the office files up to an online system that, ironically, Buzzy had suggested. Regular backups were a mainstay, but backing up to an online system that Lucie could access from anywhere? Definitely handy.

Now with Buzzy releasing another suspicious design, pressure needed to be added. *Yes, bitch, we are on to you.*

"I'll call the lawyer again. Please tell me you scanned the sketch of that vest."

Ro reached the edge of Lucie's desk, pivoted, and stomped back to the front of the shop. "Bet your tiny little ass, I did. I'm also keeping a daily log of any ideas I come up with."

"Thank you. If you're going to pace like that, you should wear a pedometer. Imagine the calories you're burning."

"You're *so* funny. It's all a joke to little miss skinny."

Lucie snorted. "I'm just saying."

The pacing stopped when Ro reached the front window. She stared out for a minute, then sprinted back to her desk, boobs bouncing, sky-high heels wobbling, and all that movement pushing her skirt to its unholy limits.

At her desk, she slowed her pace, taking care to ease into her chair. She'd learned the hard way that sitting too fast might pop a seam. The drama that day had gone to epic heights.

Having safely landed, she perched her librarian-look readers on her nose. "Joey just double-parked outside. Pretend I'm not here."

Finally, Lucie's blood pressure waved the white flag. How much of this could she take? Since the morning of the big blowout with Joey—and who the hell knew what they even fought about—the two of them had been giving each other the silent treatment. Literally not even acknowledging the other's presence.

Which made the work environment a tad awkward.

"Sorry," Lucie said, "I've been pretending you're not here for three days. It's dumb."

"Of course, it's dumb. It's a game we play to test our stubbornness. Whoever holds out the longest wins."

"Um, Ro? Games are supposed to be fun."

The doggie bells on the door jangled and Ro swiveled her chair, giving Joey her back as she pounded away on her keyboard. More than likely, there wasn't even a file open.

"Hi, Luce," her ape of a brother said as he lumbered through the door, bringing a blast of frigid air with him. December in Chicago was no joke.

Ignoring her—as well as Ro—Joey strode to the wall and snatched the next day's dog walking schedule from the folder hanging on the bulletin board.

These two dodos needed shock therapy.

"You know what?" Lucie said, "You two are the biggest dopes I know. You love each other and yet—" she paddled her hand, "—we have nonsense."

"What's this?" Joey said, waving the schedule. "No Otis? Is he okay?"

Her brother. The Otis-loving mush. "He's fine. Mrs. L will be home tomorrow. The upshot is, you'll get done an hour earlier and you and my friend over there can make up."

Her brother started for the door again. "Who?"

Terrific.

Another day in paradise.

2

____

At 1:00 the shop door swung open. In came Tim O'Brien, a man she'd grown to love with a ferocity that got Lucie's libido into high gear. Her hottie detective kept the winter months a whole lot warmer.

Today, he wore a navy suit, his wide shoulders filling out the unbuttoned jacket and grey dress shirt nicely. His badge hung at his waist along with his sidearm. *Hot, hot, hot.*

The fact that Tim was a six-foot-plus hunk of Irish burning love didn't hurt. When he came around, her heart felt...full. Happy.

"Ladies," he said.

"O'Hottie," Ro said, "what are you doing here in the middle of the day? No robbers to bust? No tickets to write?"

Tim's bottom lip rolled out, the immediate tell that he understood something extremely large had crawled up Ro's butt. "I'm a detective. I don't write tickets anymore. I was on the Southside questioning a witness. Figured I'd swing by and see Lucie on my way back to the Loop. I guess you and the big man are fighting again."

"Not again," Lucie said. "Still. It's insanity."

Tim set his hands on Lucie's desk, leaned over and gave her one of his body-zapping hello kisses.

"Blech," Ro said.

"Man," Tim whispered, "she's in a mood."

"Tell me about it. Plus, she thinks Buzzy stole another one of her designs."

"I don't think. *I know*."

Tim straightened and turned to Ro. "You got proof?"

"Right here." She whipped the printout of her sketch at him. "These are my notes and my original drawing. *And*, here's a screenshot of what was on her website. She's a lying, thieving bitch. She runs a billion-dollar company and she has to crush the little guy? I'm so done."

Again, Tim gave Lucie the raised eyebrows. *Yeah, thanks for getting her wound up, fella.*

"I'll call the lawyer again. We'll go see him and show him your evidence. Maybe we won't have to sue her. I'd like to avoid that and just settle it."

"Oh, I say we sue her. Thief that she is."

"Wow," Tim said. "Sounds like you guys are having a bad day. And here I was thinking I'd surprise you and take you to lunch."

A surprise indeed. With Tim working downtown and Lucie spending more time in the new Coco Barknell corporate office—aka the old Carlucci shoe store in her hometown—Lucie didn't often get to see him during the day. Before the Coco Barknell expansion, when Lucie handled the brunt of the dog walking, maybe she could have managed to meet up, but since the business had grown and required her to be in the office more, she didn't have the luxury of lunches out.

"I'd love that," she said.

"Have I told you," he said, "how crazy I am about you?"

Across from them, Ro made gagging noises. "Sorry. Hairball. But for the love of God, just skip lunch and get a room."

Lucie stood, shoved around Tim and stuck her tongue out at Ro. Immature, yes. But, oh well.

Refusing to be outdone, Ro returned the gesture, but couldn't keep a straight face and burst out laughing.

"Atta girl, Ro," Tim said.

Ro waved him off. "She's just too darned nice. Flip me off or something. Put a little mean into it."

That wouldn't happen. They all knew Lucie didn't like swearing. Sure she popped off every now and again, but mostly, she kept it clean.

Tim turned his back to Ro and nudged his head in her direction. *Invite her?* he mouthed.

What a guy. This was why she loved him. He came in expecting to have a quiet lunch with Lucie and now, despite Ro being crabby, he felt bad leaving her behind.

Lucie nodded. Getting away from the office might do her BFF some good. "Ro, come to lunch with us. We won't even go to Petey's if you don't want."

Two doors down, Petey's luncheonette was activity central for Lucie's father, notorious mob boss Joe Rizzo, and his cronies. Joey, when not helping Lucie, often hung out with them while managing his bookie business. Rumor had it they paid Petey a stipend every month for letting them use his place as a center of operations. Lucie stayed out of all that though. For years she'd rebelled against the mob princess moniker, fighting to rise above it by being an educated career girl. All her master's degree from Notre Dame and the subsequent job at an investment firm got her was busted back to the unemployment line—and living under her father's roof—after being downsized.

"I'll stay here," Ro said. "I'm on a diet."

A diet. Please. "Did the three-way with Ben & Jerry put you over the edge?"

Being a red-blooded man with a healthy appetite for sex, Tim's head snapped around. "Three-way?"

"Relax, killer. We're talking ice cream."

"A three-way with ice cream? I like the sound of that."

"You know," Ro said, "they're all alike. Sex and boobs. That's all they think about."

"And three-ways," Tim cracked.

Lucie poked her finger at him. "Shut it, mister." She whirled back to Ro. "And you, call my brother. Declare a truce or something. Please. I can't take you being this way. It's not like you. Just, for once, give in. Be the bigger person."

Ro curled her lip. So much for that suggestion.

"Whatever," Lucie said. "We're going to lunch. While I'm gone, stay off the internet. No more research on Buzzy's new designs. You're too keyed up. If you find anything else, you might lose it. I fear the universe won't survive."

"You are just full of the wisecracks today. Go to lunch. I'll handle the phones."

"I'm serious. No more research."

Ro held up her hand. "I won't. I swear. No research."

***

MIDWAY THROUGH THE EUPHORIA OF HER CHICKEN PARM sandwich, Lucie's phone, as Mom would say, tinkled.

Tim shoved a forkful of Petey's lasagna into his mouth and eyed her as he chewed.

"I'm not answering it."

Lemon, one of Dad's crew, sat at the table next to them, the day's *Banner-Herald* spread in front of him. He glanced over, his lips dipped into a frown. "What's that noise?"

"Lucie's phone," Dad said from the table where he and Jimmy played cards.

The phone bleeped again and Tim waved his fork at her. "You can get it."

Nope. Not doing it. Time with her man had been scarce lately and she intended on enjoying every second of this impromptu lunch.

Tinkle, tinkle.

Tinkle, tinkle.

"Ho! How am I supposed to concentrate?"

This from Jimmy, who found endless usage for the word ho.

Dad threw his cards on the table. "Jesus Christmas. I'm banning cell phones in Petey's. As of now leave them in your cars. You hear?"

As if a bunch of sixty-year-old mob guys received a lot of texts?

"Luce," Tim said, "please. Just answer the damned thing and shut it up."

Wiping her hands on a napkin, she dug the phone from her purse. "I'm sorry. I can't imagine what's so urgent." She poked the screen. A text from Sissy Washington, the managing director of Pups for Progress, the non-profit hosting the fashion show Coco Barknell and Buzzy were designing garments for. "Ah. Sissy Washington. Should have known."

"She's the dog charity lady, right?"

"Yep. Together, she and Ro create enough drama to keep Broadway theatres profitable." She read the first text. A question about Ro's sanity.

Debatable, that.

She scrolled to the second text. A screenshot of a tweet. The third text, another screenshot. The fourth, yet another screenshot with a message.

WTF?

Tim shoveled the last of the lasagna and dropped his fork. "What is it?"

"I don't know." Lucie used her fingers to enlarge the screenshot. "Oh, no."

Please, no.

"Luce?"

Was it possible to feel her entire body go numb at once? She paused for a second and took stock. Yes. Definitely possible. She scraped her chair back, the annoying sound sending her father's crew into theatrics.

"Ho! My ears," Jimmy said.

"I have to go," Lucie said.

Tim's eyebrows hitched. "What?"

"I have to go. Can you pay the check?"

"Sure. What's up?"

"I'm about to murder my best friend and I don't want my detective boyfriend to witness it."

Lucie threw the shop door open, propped her hands on her hips so she wouldn't strangle her best friend, and forced herself to stay calm.

Calm, calm, calm.

At least until Ro came out of the break room, requisite container of Ben & Jerry's in hand. It had to stop. All of it. Fighting with Joey, fighting with Buzzy, the ice cream binges. If Lucie didn't control this situation, Ro's life—professional and personal—would derail.

"Hey," Ro said, "how was lunch?"

I'll tell you how lunch was... "You are a thieving *beyotch*?"

Two more spoonfuls of Rocky Road met their demise in Ro's mouth before she gestured wildly with the spoon. "I was worked up. Heat of the moment and all that. I deleted it."

"After it was retweeted thirty thousand times."

More Rocky Road. "It might be up to forty. But who's counting?"

"I'm counting! Are you insane?" Lucie waved her arms. "Forget that. Clearly, you're insane, because I specifically remember telling you to stay off the internet. You swore to me."

Ro pondered another scoop of ice cream. "It's been a heck of a day so far. That witch Buzzy stealing another of my designs and Joey ignoring me might have been too much."

"So you lose your mind on Twitter?"

"Well, it wasn't exactly like that. I needed a distraction. Work always helps, so I figured, you know, I'd get back to my routine."

Her routine got her into a smack down on Twitter? "This, I can't wait to hear."

"I had to check our social media accounts—and, yes, I know that's the internet—but I had to respond to any questions or comments."

Okay, that, Lucie understood. Each day at noon, Ro logged on and spent a good thirty minutes talking with peeps online. Recently, they'd implemented an online shop and that meant getting their products out there. In the three weeks since the launch, their online sales had tripled. Definitely needed to give Ro credit for that.

How that turned into calling Buzzy a thieving bitch, Lucie didn't quite grasp.

Rather than bludgeon her closest friend, Lucie rolled one hand, indicating Ro should continue talking. Fast.

Another mound of Rocky Road went into her mouth and she waggled the spoon. "I started with Twitter today, scrolling my lists of favorites. And there it was."

"What?"

"The chinchilla vest. Our vest!"

"Oh, my God. Why didn't you just get out of there?"

"I tried. But...but...there were a bunch of tweets talking about how great the vest was. You know how I am. That rage just built and built." Ro's mouth twisted into a sneer. "And *built*, Luce."

Lucie shoved her fingers against her eyes, checking to make sure they hadn't A) burst from her skull and B) started bleeding. Buzzy, with her millions of followers, had retweeted someone's praise of "her" fabulous new Chinchilla vest.

An image filled Lucie's mind.

Bradley Cooper—hey, a girl could dream—escorting a chinchilla-clad Ninja Bitch Shih-Tzu hottie down the runway while the audience went wild.

Over *Buzzy's* so-called design.

Except it was Ro's design, one she'd spent weeks perfecting only to have it snatched. Without even a simple credit. Ro shoved another scoop of ice cream into her mouth, and a trickle of understanding knocked Lucie's fury to a low boil.

"Luce, I'm sorry. All I could think about was outing that bitch. I'm so sorry."

And then Ro, pillar of strength and possessor of all things mighty, burst into tears. Not just everyday crying either. This was a full on, face twisted, mouth wide enough to drive a truck through jag.

Cripes. Lucie threw her arms up. "Whoa, don't cry. Please."

"I was just so mad." She jabbed the spoon at Lucie. "Between the stolen designs and your dopey brother, everything feels out of control right now."

In went another giant scoop of Rocky Road. Her BFF had lost it. Completely.

It had to stop.

Lucie strode toward Ro, snagged the pint of ice cream and the spoon, and took them to the break room.

"What are you doing?"

"Enough with this."

"Luce, don't."

"Oh, I'm doing it."

Yes, she was. Right to the sink she went, slapping on the faucet as she pried the ice cream from the container.

Behind her, Ro gasped and—*whap*—shoved her. Hard. Lucie let out a yip. When the heck had Ro ever done *that*? To Lucie anyway. The container flew, making a wide arc. Ro reached up, her greedy, desperate fingers stretched wide, but Lucie rebounded and caught herself on the sink. Gaining her balance again, she used the sink for leverage and—*whoop*—pushed off, launching herself at Ro. Seconds before the pint landed, Lucie walloped her, knocking her flat on her ass.

Holy cow.

The pint landed on the tile, the remaining contents splattering in a chocolately mess. The two of them scrambled, then dove for the pint, landing in a heap on the ground.

Then Lucie went airborne, her legs cycling as temper sparked. She swung her head around and spotted Tim, arm clasped around her waist, hauling her backward.

"Put me down." She pointed at Ro. "Touch that pint and I'll murder you."

Ro gasped again, dropped the ice cream and slammed her hands on the floor.

Tim set Lucie down, but body blocked her before she could swoop around him. "What the hell is wrong with you two?" He bent down and scooped up the battered Rocky Road. "You've got to be kidding me. You're fighting over *ice cream*."

"She started it," Lucie said.

Oh, very mature.

Still on the floor, Ro gave her the stink eye. "You were washing my ice cream down the drain. I paid good money for that."

Come on. *That's* what she went with? "Now it's about the money? Fine. I'll reimburse you."

Ever the gentleman, Tim reached a hand to Ro and helped her off the ground. "Are you okay?"

She gave her battle weary, but still intact skirt a tug. How that thing hadn't split in half was beyond Lucie. Ro straightened the sleeves of her blouse. Lucie held off mentioning the chocolate stain just above Ro's left boob. No way that would come out of silk. That shirt became the only victim in the Rocky Road war.

"I'm fine," Ro said. "Just...mad. And, well, embarrassed."

Tim set his hand on her shoulder and squeezed. "Don't be. You guys have always been nuts. Nothing shocks me anymore."

The look Ro gave him should have melted the skin from his bones. Being an intelligent man, he stepped back.

"Tough guy," Lucie muttered.

With Tim out of the way, Ro put her arms out and

wrapped Lucie in a hug. "I'm sorry, Luce. Please forgive me. Please. I'd never hurt you. You know I love you."

"Of course I forgive you. Are you kidding? You beat up Tiffy Nelson for me in the third grade. I love you too. I just want you to be happy. If arguing with my brother does this to you, something has to change."

"I know. It drives us both crazy, but we're too stubborn to give in."

The much taller Ro, ducked her head to Lucie's shoulder and a chunk of Lucie's heart gave way. Even when Ro's rat bastard, stripper-banging ex-husband had humiliated her, Ro hadn't crumpled like this.

Damned Joey.

Ro let out a little sniffle. "I hate myself right now. I can't stop eating and I'm miserable."

"Call him. Make this craziness stop."

"I'll do it. I'll call him."

Tonight Lucie would get on her knees and thank God and every angel for making this miracle happen.

Ro stood tall, gave up a watery smile. "I might have to kill him though. Just so you know."

"Whatever it takes. I'll even help."

"Uh," Tim said. "Time for me to go. Is it safe to leave you two? I mean, we're not gonna have a crime scene here, right?"

Funny man.

Lucie whirled on him just as Ro said, "Beat it, O'Hottie."

He whipped off that sweet Irish-boy smile Lucie loved so much and all the bluster left her. How could she mouth off to such a hunk?

"You're lucky you're cute," she said.

"I know." He popped a kiss on her lips. "See ya later. Love you."

"Love you too."

"Ew," Ro said.

After dumping the remaining ice cream, Ro followed Lucie from the break room. "I'm sorry about the tweet-gone-wild."

Tweet-gone-wild. Good one.

"Let's chalk it up to a bad day. We'll have some damage control, but as long as you deleted it, we'll be fine."

"I'll apologize to her."

That's all they needed. Buzzy would whip out that *I'm-so-arrogant* attitude she wore like a second skin and Ro might hurl her Louis Vuitton at her.

Lucie held up a hand. "Wait on that. I'll talk to the lawyer and see what he advises. I'm not sure we should be apologizing for anything if we're about to sue her."

"We're suing her? Really?"

"I talked to Tim about it at lunch. It looks like she's making money on your designs. At the very least, she needs to compensate us. If we can prove our case, we'll demand payment. If she doesn't agree, we'll sue. Besides, she *is* a thieving beyotch."

Ro smacked her hand on the desk. "Exactly!"

"Just, please, no communication of any sort with Buzzy. Even if you have to remove her from your social media feed, stay away. Got it?"

"Yes, ma'am. No Buzzy."

"Good. Now call my brother before someone gets hurt."

3

———

THAT EVENING, WHILE MOM PUT THE FINISHING TOUCHES ON her famous pot roast, Lucie did her part by setting the dining room table. Dad and Joey, of course, did their parts by sitting in the adjoining living room in front of the television.

Some things would never change in this household. The women doing the domestic duties was one of them. Something she didn't have to worry about with Tim. He'd been living on his own long enough that he didn't have a problem strapping on an apron or washing dishes. When Lucie went to his place for dinner, they both cooked, they both cleaned up, they both watched television.

Together.

The front door flew open and Lucie scooted to the end of the table hoping to see her BFF making her usual grand entrance. When Ro walked into the house, stillness suddenly turned to movement and everything got hectic in a totally fun way. Usually. With this Joey-Ro war, who knew what Ro's crazy energy would bring.

After the epic meltdown earlier, Ro had promised to

make nice with Joey and her appearance was a sign. A good one, hopefully, that meant Lucie's life getting a whole lot simpler because her vice president of sales wasn't pulling threesomes with Ben & Jerry.

All around, Lucie—and Coco Barknell—needed Ro's head back in the game.

"Hellooo," Ro called as she strode into the living room on her mile-high stilettos.

Even twelve-point-five pounds heavier, Ro was a stunner. Tonight her wavy dark hair fell around perfectly sculpted cheekbones. She'd topped it all off by changing into a mini-skirt that showed off her long legs. All, of course, under a mink coat.

Ro, no matter her size, would always be a mankiller. She simply had that way about her. As if on cue, Joey's head swung around and he fixed his gaze on her as she moved toward him. When she reached him, she smacked him on the back of the head.

"Ow!"

"We need to talk. Now. Hi, Mr. R." She bent low and pecked Dad on the cheek.

"Hiya," he said, shaking his head over the smack. "You're a wacky broad."

"Yeah, well, apparently, that's what your son needs. Hi, Luce."

Lucie set the last fork, the fifth one for Ro, on the table. "Hi. I had a feeling you'd be here."

"Yep. And if your brother doesn't get his giant ass off that couch and talk to me, I'm staying anyway. He'll have to look at me all through dinner."

Dad leaned over and backhanded Joey on the arm. "Why aren't you talking to her?"

"Why is everyone hitting me tonight?"

Lucie took that one. "Maybe because you deserve it?"

"Shut it, you," Joey warned, then addressed Dad. "We had a fight. And she's not talking to me either. Don't let her bulldoze you. She's not innocent in all this."

"Jesus Christmas," Dad said. "I got an entire crew down at Petey's that doesn't give me an ulcer like you two."

With the bunch her father led, that was saying something. But Lucie didn't like to think about her father's "day job." Joe Rizzo had saddled her with never-ending mob princess jokes that she'd spent most of her adult life trying to rise above.

And it was a brutal climb.

"Five minutes," Mom hollered from the kitchen.

Ro glanced at Lucie and she waggled her thumb in Joey's direction. After the day they'd had, Lucie wanted a reasonably subdued dinner—always a challenge in the Rizzo home. If Ro didn't get moving on Operation Joey, they'd create a boatload of tension at the table.

Fully embracing Lucie's request, Ro stepped in front of Joey, who had yet to move, and held her coat open, giving him a view of her blouse. The one that included the extra button undone and revealing a mountain of cleavage. Really dirty pool. She knew the effect she had on him.

Plus, she was blocking the television.

"Oh, boy," Dad said.

Mom poked her head into the dining room. "What's going on?"

"Nothing. Joey and Ro are making up."

"They're fighting again?"

"Yes."

Mom rolled her eyes and went back to the kitchen. Life in the Rizzo household.

Ro grabbed Joey by the wrist, dragging his butt up. "We'll

go upstairs and settle this. Either that or I'm walking out. And I won't be walking back in."

That got the big man's attention. He stood in front of Ro, staring down at her. As tall as Ro was in her heels, Joey still had a good four inches on her. "What?"

"You heard me. I can't do this anymore. Ben & Jerry's stock is going up because of me. Pretty soon my ass won't fit through the door."

Again, Dad shook his head. He hated when women swore. Well, too bad. Ro was right. On all fronts.

But her brother was stubborn. He might need a little more of a push and Lucie was never one to shy away from irritating her brother. The way she figured it, he'd tormented her from the time they were kids and deserved whatever he got. She still smarted from that time he challenged her to a pull-up contest and then left her hanging from the tree branch, screaming until her voice gave out. At the time, she'd been too afraid to let go and possibly break her legs on the fall.

Joey. Mr. Wonderful.

"Listen," Lucie said, "we had a rough day and I'm not up for any drama tonight. Ro is taking the high road. Be a man and talk to her."

Ro gave him a shove. "Let's go."

He marched to the stairs, flipping Lucie the bird behind Dad's back. Which of course, she happily flipped right back.

Perfect. At least there'd been some progress.

"Lucie," Mom called. "Your phone is ringing. Well, not ringing. Tinkling."

"It's probably a text."

"Ooh," Mom said, "It's still going. You're so popular."

"What's all the yelling about?" Dad yelled. "I'm watching my program here."

Lucie needed to move out. The insanity of this household, even with Joey living in his own place, was too much. By day, Lucia Rizzo was an ambitious entrepreneur building what she hoped would someday be a Fortune 500 company. When she stepped through the front door of her parents' home, she somehow time warped back to being twelve years old. The yearning to be on her own again nudged her constantly.

Before being downsized out of her banking job, she'd had her own apartment in Chicago. Living the life. She'd been in love back then, enjoying her time with Frankie, the son of her father's closest friend and the first boy she'd ever gotten starry eyed over. Except, in the end, they couldn't make it work. She'd always care for him, but what she had with Tim was...different.

Simpler.

No drama. No splitting up and getting back together. No one taking bets on when the next break would happen.

Her relationship with Tim was the adult version of falling in love.

Mom peeked through the kitchen doorway and held Lucie's still-*tinkling* phone out. "Please deal with this before I throw it outside."

"Yes, ma'am. Sorry."

What the heck could be going on? She tapped the screen, spotted six messages. Three from Sissy Washington. The other three came from staff members at Pups for Progress.

Apparently, there was some kind of doggie fashion crisis. Lucie tapped Sissy's first message.

Turn on your TV. Breaking news. Buzzy=Dead.

Clearly, Buzzy had done something to piss off Sissy also.

The woman was on a roll today. Lucie tapped the next message.

Did you see it?

And the third message.

Where are you?

Yikes. A girl couldn't leave her phone for five minutes.

"Dad," Lucie said, "I need the television a second."

Having no doubt her father would protest, Lucie scooped the remote from the sofa cushion and flipped to the local Chicago news station.

"Baby girl, I was watching that."

"I know. I'll change it back."

"You know," he said, "I don't understand. A man can't watch his own damned television in peace around here. I should go back to the joint. There, I had peace."

"You also had a lack of sunshine and—oh, yeah—freedom. Oh, my God!"

Scrolling at the bottom of the screen under a bright red breaking news banner was a report of a homicide.

Buzzy Sneider's homicide.

Buzzy=Dead.

Sissy wasn't kidding.

Lucie followed the scroll, lost in stunned disbelief as it ticked by. Buzzy was...gone.

"Roseanne!"

"Again with the yelling?" This from Dad who swung his head up, his face a twisted mass of frustration.

She couldn't worry about Dad right now. She raced to the stairs, took them two at a time, and halted midway when Ro appeared at the top.

"What happened?"

"It's Buzzy."

"That bitch. What'd she do now? Tell me she swiped another one of our designs. I swear to God I'll kill her."

"Too late. Someone already did."

Ro cocked her head. "I'm sorry, Luce, but trying to talk sense into your thick-headed brother must have exhausted my working brain cells. Did you just say someone *killed* Buzzy?"

"Your brain cells are fine." Lucie headed back down the stairs, waving Ro to follow. "I got a text from Sissy. It's on the news. There's no info yet, but it's scrolling on the bottom."

Ro hit the landing, her long hair flying as she made the turn. "What happened?"

"Sssh, here it is." Lucie grabbed the remote again and turned the volume up.

Still in his chair, Dad waved a hand. "Who's this Buzzy broad?"

"Ssssh."

But Ro couldn't resist. "She's the thieving witch who stole my designs."

"Someone whacked her?"

"Dad. Hush! I need to hear this."

Everyone went quiet. A minor miracle in this house. Just in case, Lucie turned up the volume as the anchor tossed it over to a reporter standing in front of a police barricade.

"That's Buzzy's house," Ro said.

"Ssssh...let's hear this."

"Buzzy Sneider, a local celebrity and home decor guru known for her hugely popular reality show, was discovered deceased by her older sister at approximately 5:45 pm. This appears to be a homicide, but detectives are still inside the home and no details have been released. We're expecting a statement from Foo-Foo Entertainment, Buzzy's company,

any time now. We'll bring that to you live as it happens. Back to the studio."

"I can't believe it," Ro said, "I was just—" She stopped, shook her head.

Lucie handed the remote back to Dad. "You were just what?"

"Roseanne," Joey yelled from upstairs. "Are we done?"

Mom swung into the dining room carrying a huge platter of pot roast. "Dinner's ready. Everyone at the table."

The thud of Joey's giant feet hitting the stairs nearly shook the house. "Smells great, ma. I'm starved."

On his way by, he smacked Ro on the rear. "Glad we straightened that out. I kinda missed you."

But Ro simply stood next to Lucie, her eyes still on the television. "This is crazy. She's *dead*?"

"Totally crazy. And we were about to sue her."

"Oh, Luce. Not to talk business at a time like this, but that's going to be a mess."

Lucie let that sink in. She could drop the idea of the lawsuit, but last she checked, Buzzy's website indicated the designs she'd swiped from Coco Barknell were on back order and still selling for $149.95 each. Which meant Foo-Foo was making a boatload on them.

And Lucie couldn't stomach that. Fair was fair. Coco Barknell, no matter this tragedy, deserved to be compensated.

Tim.

He's who she needed now. Always the voice of reason. Someone to talk through options with. He'd have answers. Whether or not he'd share those answers was debatable. One of his finer qualities was his steadfast dedication to being a police officer. An honorable, straight-arrow detective who rarely, if ever, shared information about cases.

She loved that about him. Even when her father, scary mob boss Joe Rizzo, wanted him to spill information regarding a piece of memorabilia Lucie had been suspected of stealing, Tim didn't compromise. He found a way to help Lucie without jeopardizing his ethics. Or his career.

"Lucie," Mom said, "please."

Food. The idea of it sent a bout of nausea swimming in Lucie's stomach. She'd have to choke it down though.

"Call O'Hottie," Ro said.

"Exactly what I was thinking. After dinner, we'll see if we can track him down. Maybe get some answers."

AFTER CLEANING UP THE DINNER DISHES, RO AND JOEY took off to whereabouts unknown—more than likely to one of the bedrooms to make up for lost time. *Blech!* Lucie didn't like thinking about her brother and her BFF doing the nasty.

Just gross.

Instead of dwelling on disgusting thoughts, she wandered up to her bedroom, the one with the same princess furniture from elementary school.

She dropped on the bed and studied the swirl design on her dresser. Maybe it was time to move out. To bust her big girl furniture out of storage and get an apartment again. Something downtown. Closer to Tim.

Or was that moving too fast? They'd already exchanged I-love-yous. Many times—*eh-hem*—so that was promising. She wouldn't rush things though. Slow, slow, slow.

Yet, during times of crisis, the first person she thought of was her hunky, red-haired detective.

She scrolled her contacts, found O'Hottie, and tapped the screen.

"Hey, Luce."

Uh-oh. His voice carried that breathy sound it took on when he was in a rush. Or stressed.

"Hi. Is this a bad time?"

"No. It's good. I'm walking to my car. I'm working a case."

"I won't keep you. I just saw the news about Buzzy. I can't believe it."

"It's nuts. The brass has all the homicide guys on alert. Detectives outside of homicide too. All hands on deck."

Not a shock, based on Buzzy's celebrity status, but considering the number of homicides in Chicago, that was a lot of detectives.

"Are you on this? Do they have any leads?"

"Luce—"

Lucie curled her lip. Leave it to her to find an honorable detective. "I know, I know. You can't comment. I had to try."

He chuckled. One thing about Tim, he found the lighter side in just about anything. Cops had that twisted gallows humor that kept them from going insane over the day-to-day depravity they witnessed.

"I'd expect nothing less. Doesn't matter anyway. I don't know anything more than what the media has. You okay with this whole thing?"

Lucie flopped back on her bed. "Me? I'm fine. I feel horrible for her family. Lorraine lives right next door. That's got to be horrible. Buzzy might have been a thief, but she didn't deserve this. It's sad."

"Yeah, it is. Babe, I gotta run. But listen, you know how this works. They're gonna be looking at everything and everybody."

Which meant... "You're telling me to expect a call from a detective."

"I don't know for sure, but that's what I'd do. I'd round up anyone she had a beef with and question them. SOP."

SOP. Standard Operating Procedure. Tim's favorite acronym.

Lucie hadn't thought about being questioned. The shock of Buzzy's death had numbed her to that little factoid. *Ugh.* How the hell did she always wind up involved in this stuff?

"They can ask me anything. As *usual* I have nothing to hide."

Tim let out a snort. "Good. I can't take another one of your adventures so soon after the Cock Heads."

"Hey! It's not like I ask for this stuff to happen. I just have rotten luck. And don't make fun of the Cock Heads. They're nice people. In a goofy sort of way."

Lucie had met the Cock Heads while investigating the theft of The Max, a priceless dress from a famous sci-fi flick featuring peacocks that take over an island. Lucie had become a suspect and some of the fan club's members had helped solved the crime. And clear Lucie. As a result, she liked to attend Cock Head meetings to catch up with her new friends.

"Okay," Tim said. "I won't make fun of them. Much."

"Whatever, detective. Since you're not around to tickle the ivories with me tonight, I may, in fact, go to a Cock Head meeting. I think there's one in Lincoln Park."

"Where's Ro?"

"She and Joey made up. They're most likely holed up somewhere banging. The pervs."

Again Tim laughed. "You're so damned cute, Lucie."

"It's a curse."

"I know. Alright, I gotta fly. If you go to a meeting tonight, be careful. Call me when you're on your way home so I know you're okay."

"I will. You be careful too. I don't want to have to rough anyone up because they hurt my man."

"Yes, ma'am. I'll talk to you later. Love you."

"Love you too."

She disconnected and tossed her phone on the bed, stretching her arms and legs wide.

Someone pounded on her door so hard, it nearly shook the bed. Had to be Dad and his giant fist. Lucie levered up just as her father stuck his head in.

"Dad, were you eavesdropping on my call with Tim?"

"Not the whole thing."

But, yes, he'd probably heard that line about Joey and Ro banging each other. Lucie's cheeks suddenly got hot. She so had to move out.

"Listen, baby girl. I'm putting a call into Willie."

"Why?"

"Whaddya mean why? This broad who stole from you is dead. You don't think the cops are gonna be on you? I guarantee in the next 12 hours they'll come for you. Just let your old man handle it. This is why I keep Willie on retainer. You never know when this type of thing will happen."

Sometimes a girl didn't need to think about her father having a criminal defense attorney at his beck-and-call. Then again, lately Willie had been her lawyer more than her father's. So much for rising above being a mob princess.

"Thanks, Dad. I appreciate it. Tim said detectives might have questions for me, but I was in the office all afternoon so I wasn't anywhere near Buzzy."

"I know." He waved a hand. "Don't worry. We got plenty of guys that'll say they saw you."

"Dad, I don't need them to lie for me. I was in the office."

"A little insurance never hurts."

This life. Unbelievable. "No insurance, Dad. Please. I won't need it. The UPS guy came in at 4:00 with a shipment I signed for. My alibi is rock solid."

THE FOLLOWING MORNING, LUCIE RUMMAGED THROUGH THE clump of pens in her top drawer, trying desperately to find a red one. Did pens procreate? Because she wasn't quite sure how she wound up with so many of them.

"Stop with the noise," Ro said from her desk. "What are you doing?"

Someone was crabby. Again. It appeared, given the luggage under Ro's eyes, she and Joey had a long night.

"I have five million pens and not a red one to be found."

Lucie gathered all the pens from the drawer and dumped them on top of the desk, each landing with a smack louder than should have been feasibly possible.

Flick. Something bounced off the back of Lucie's computer monitor and landed on the tile. She peeped over the side of the desk and spotted the red pen.

"Did you just throw that at me?"

"You said you were looking for a red pen. Can you be quiet now? I've got three days to come up with new designs for the fashion show."

"We don't need new designs. We're still going with the ones Buzzy stole. God rest her soul."

"That thieving bitch. God rest her soul."

Temporarily ignoring the pen on the floor, Lucie went to work sorting the mess on her desk. The task, the mundane trappings of organizing each by color, was oddly relaxing. This whole Buzzy mess had rattled her. Any minute now, she expected a detective to march in and confront her, the woman threatening to sue a recently murdered celebrity. Oh, she could see the headline now: Mob Princess Suspected of Murder.

Somehow, it always came down to her being Joe Rizzo's kid.

Lucie shook it off. No time for that now. "I can't believe she's dead."

"She must have really pissed someone off. And, hello, the media isn't saying boo about how she died."

"Asphyxiation."

"Well, yeah, but that could be anything. Did someone strangle her, put a pillow over her head, what?"

Lucie gathered all the blue pens into a pile and counted them. "Fourteen blue pens. Who needs fourteen blue pens?"

Another red projectile flew across the room, this time dangerously close to her face. "Quit it! It's all fun and games until someone puts out an eye."

Finally, Ro got up and stomped over to Lucie's desk. Today's ensemble included a red skirt that may have been even tighter than yesterday's. Good thing Ro didn't buy cheap. If she did, those skirts would be shredded from stress by now.

She shoved the pens aside. "Stop with this a minute. Or let me help you."

There's a thought. "Put rubber bands around these blue ones. They all need to go back to the supply closet. The black ones too."

They worked together, bundling the small mountains of pens, and then walked them back to the break room supply closet.

At the closet, Ro relieved Lucie of her bundles. "I'll put these away."

"I've got it. You're busy."

Ro waved her off. "I'm good. Go back to your spread-sheet. I need some mindless work while I noodle design ideas. Beat it."

This might be a lucky break. If Ro stayed in the supply room, Lucie wouldn't be face to face with her dramatics. She'd consider it a vacation. "Okay, but call me if you need help."

"Luce, it's not brain surgery. I'm guessing I can handle it."

Totally crabby today. "Yeesh. Don't take it out on me."

"I'm sorry. I'm just tired. The fight with Joey wore me out. I think this is the hangover."

"But you're good now?"

Ro shrugged. "I guess. Of course, he's not planning on giving up bookmaking any time soon, so the whole ordeal was a big waste of energy. I don't know, Luce. I love him, but sometimes I could kill him."

"You think that makes you special? We all feel that way."

At that, Ro laughed. "Go back to work." She looked up at the shelves with a critical eye. "You know, this has gotten out of control. The staples and paper clips should be together. And why don't we have paper and notepads on the same shelf? I'm going to get us organized here. Maybe it'll spur some creative juices."

Lucie headed back to her desk ready to tackle the following year's budget in peace. If her projections were correct, she might be able to move out of Villa Rizzo. Even if the expansion from Mom's dining room into their current space had created additional expenses.

The bells on the door jangled and Dad strolled through. In keeping with his reputation for natty attire, he wore dress slacks, a crisp button down shirt, and his short hair perfectly groomed. Her father, a fanatic about his personal appearance, had always been handsome. The way he told it, half the women who entered his orbit were attracted to him. Lucie didn't know about all that, but Dad had a way about him.

This would be the first of many visits from him throughout the day. The interruptions drove Lucie half crazy, but she tried to be patient. As Joey had once pointed out, the idea of walking down the street, for a man who'd been incarcerated for two years, meant freedom.

"Baby girl," Dad said, "any sign of cops yet? I've had the boys on lookout, but...nothing. Willie is on his way. Just in case we need him."

Willie may have been Dad's defense attorney, but lately most of his billable hours had been spent on Lucie.

"Not yet, Dad. They may not even question me. And why are you spending money on Willie if we're not sure detectives will even want to talk to me."

Dad gave her a look. "They'll be here. Bet on it. Plus, Lemon knows a guy who knows a guy. He's homicide at area three."

Lucie held her hands up. "Don't tell me."

"Why?"

Why? For one, he'd obtained that information through one of his lowlife cohorts. Not that Lemon was a lowlife. He was, in fact, a decent man. Considering he made his living shaking people down. But still, whoever these friends of friends were, she wanted no part of it.

"Dad, my boyfriend is a Chicago detective. I don't want to know anything about this case that's not public knowledge. People might think Tim leaked information, and I'm not doing that to him."

Her father rolled her eyes. "Here we go with the big shot

attitude. Fine. I won't tell you how this broad died. I'll keep it to myself."

Oh, dangling that catnip was a low blow.

"You know how she died?"

That, Lucie had to admit, was impressive. Whoever this contact was, he or she had taken a risk sharing highly under-wraps information.

Dad grinned. "You said you didn't want to know."

So not fair. Of course she wanted to know. Backpedal, backpedal, backpedal. "Let me clarify. If you've obtained this knowledge by sneaky means, I don't want to know."

"What sneaky? Someone told a guy who told a guy. How's that sneaky?"

Ro poked her head out from the back room. "*I* want to know. And I have no issues about where it came from. Tell me."

Dad spun back. "She was asphyxiated."

"We knew that. *How* was she asphyxiated?"

A filthy smile dragged across Dad's face. "Hold on to your panties, girls."

What? Since when did her father talk like that? Everyone in Lucie's life was going insane.

"Someone," he continued, "killed her with an atomic wedgie."

The shop went silent for at least thirty seconds while Dad swung his head from Ro to Lucie to Ro again. They both waited—patiently—for the punch line. Dad enjoyed the more-than-occasional twisted joke. Sometimes the stories he told sounded so realistic you didn't know he was stringing you along until he made up a goofy ending and burst out laughing.

This time? No laughing.

"Get it?" he asked. "Panties? Wedgie?

"Just stop it," Lucie said. "How did it really happen?"

"I'm not kidding." He smacked his chest then held his hand up. "Swear on my mother's grave. Atomic wedgie."

"Oh, my God," Ro muttered.

Lucie turned to her. "I'm not even sure what that is. How does my *father* know?"

Ro waggled one hand. "It's when someone gives you a wedgie, but they pull the waistband so high up it goes over your head."

"Seriously," Lucie said, "someone can die from a wedgie?"

Dad wrapped one hand around his neck and made gagging noises. "It strangled her. Whoever did it, somehow pulled the waistband up and around her neck. It cut off her air supply. She got clocked with something first though. That knocked her out and then she got wedgied."

"Ew." Ro scrunched her nose. "That has to be horrible."

She disappeared back into the storeroom and Lucie spun to her laptop. "I can't even picture that. I need to see this. Let me Google it."

Movement in front of the shop caught Lucie's attention. She glanced up to see two men emerging from a Ford identical to the one Tim drove while on duty. Plus, the number of dents were a dead giveaway.

Cops.

Lucie faced front to alert her father, but he was already on his way to the door. "Keep your mouth shut. I'll see if Willie is here."

He swung the door open just as the detectives reached it. Dad didn't bother holding the door for them and walked right through. "Her lawyer is on the way. She's not talking."

Great. Excellent way to kick things off.

One of the detectives grabbed the door before it closed and then exchanged a look with his partner.

"Gentlemen." Lucie rose from her chair. "Come in. Please. Ignore my father."

Shouldn't be a hardship considering the relationship between cops and Joe Rizzo. There wouldn't be a Christmas gift exchange any time soon.

"Thank you," the older detective said.

Between the slicked back dark hair, black slacks, and a crew neck sweater topped off with a sport coat, this man reminded her of every detective she'd ever seen on television.

The second detective was younger. Not exactly fresh-faced, but he didn't have the hard-earned grit and wrinkles of his partner. Like Tim, the younger one wore a decent suit. His blond hair was cut military style—high and tight—and gave him that commanding presence needed for police work.

Lucie waved them to the conference table. "Have a seat."

"Thank you. We'd like to ask—"

"I know," Lucie said. "You want to ask me some questions. Given my business dealings with Buzzy, I anticipated this and intend on cooperating fully. I'd like to have legal counsel present though. I hope you don't mind waiting."

Well, even if they did, too bad. Not that she had anything to hide, but this was a murder case. Lucie wasn't taking any chances. Even on her best day, she might have an attack of nerves and blurt something that could be misconstrued.

The two men exchanged another look. This one screaming of puzzlement.

"Ms. Rizzo," the older one said, "we're not here for you."

Huh? Lucie rolled her bottom lip out. "You're not?"

"No, ma'am."

"I assumed..." Well, no need to go into that. "All right. My mistake."

Maybe they were friends of Tim's or something. *Maybe* they weren't here regarding Buzzy at all. They could be stopping in to inquire about dog walking or—and wouldn't this be a kick?—to order a custom doggie coat.

This is what a life lived as the daughter of a notorious mob boss got her. She'd been conditioned to believe the police meant trouble.

"I'm sorry, gentlemen. My mistake. What can I do for you?"

"We're here for Roseanne Buccarelli."

4

———

All Lucie's deliberating and sleep loss over being questioned about Buzzy's death and they weren't even here for her? Somehow, that didn't seem fair.

They should at least ask her a few questions. Make all that stress worthwhile.

"*Roseanne*," she said. "Really?"

The Tim-wannabe jerked his head. "Yes, ma'am,"

"I don't understand."

The men exchanged another look. Without a doubt, they thought she was nuts. *Get a grip here, Luce.*

She lifted her hands. "I'm sorry. I thought...Is this about —" No. She shouldn't say anything. Not one peep. "Roseanne is in the back. I'll, um, just go grab her."

"Thank you."

Moving at a decent pace, Lucie swung into the closet. Ro had pulled everything from the two top shelves and spread it all on the floor.

She shook a box of paper clips at Lucie. "I'm telling you, this is a hot-ass mess. How did we let it get this bad?"

Lucie smacked at the box, knocking it to the floor and sending paper clips flying.

"Hey! What was that for? *You're* cleaning that up."

"There are two detectives here."

Ro's eyebrows shot up. "Already? Wow. That didn't take long."

No kidding.

"I know. A shocker. Here's another one for you. They're not here for me. They want you."

Ro took a second with that one, her mouth partly open as if words were about to come out, but somehow couldn't find their way. She lifted her gaze, peering over Lucie's shoulder. "*Me?*"

"They're out front." Making sure they hadn't followed her, Lucie arched back, peeping out to the main part of the shop. The young detective gave her a little finger wave. Yep. Still there. She went back to Ro. "I bet they saw that tweet you sent."

Ro pushed around her. "Don't start about the tweet. Let's just see what they want."

Shoulders thrown back, she marched into the hallway, her long legs leaving Lucie's much shorter ones in the dust.

"Dad went to get Willie. I don't think—"

"Ms. Buccarelli," the geezer detective said. "We have some questions to ask you regarding your relationship with Buzzy Sneider."

"I didn't have a relationship with her. We were business associates."

Lucie caught up to Ro, grabbed her elbow, and squeezed tight enough to break a bone. "As I was about to say, I think you should wait for Willie."

Because, hello! They had a murder investigation going here.

"Who's Willie?" the Tim wannabe asked.

"Lawyer," Lucie said. "Willie Clay."

Geezer rolled his eyes. "Terrific. He handles all the mob guys."

Ooooh, that was just rude. Lucie shredded him—at least she hoped—with a sneer. "He handles a variety of clients. *Including* a few bad cops."

Hey, she could do tit for tat with anyone. She wasn't Joe Rizzo's kid for nothing.

Ro flipped her hair back. "What. *Ever*. Luce, see where he is and let's get this over with."

She spun around, headed for the conference table, and —never one to fear pulling out the big guns—may have opened an extra button on her blouse as she went.

"No, ma'am."

"First of all, don't call me ma'am. Roseanne is fine. Stand if you want, but I'm sitting."

"Ms. Buccarelli," the younger detective said, "we're not doing this here. You need to come with us."

Wait one second. Ro? Downtown? Lucie had a sudden vision of her BFF locked in an interrogation room—an *interview* room, as Tim liked to call it—while two detectives tried to pry a confession out of her.

Not. A. Chance.

In the mood Ro had been in, total bloodbath. She'd wind up in jail just for having a smart mouth.

"That's not happening," Lucie said.

All three of them turned to her, but the geezer was the only one to laugh. "Believe me, it's happening, sweetheart." He waggled two fingers at Ro. "You can grab your coat or purse or whatever."

Sweetheart? What the heck? She glanced down at her jeans and tennis shoes. Eh, maybe she did look like a twelve-year-old. Apparently, the stink eye she'd given him wasn't all that intimidating.

"How long will this take?" Ro wanted to know.

Again, the detectives exchanged a glance. What was this silent communication they had going? Cop non-speak. Lucie would have to ask Tim about that. But really, how the heck was a girl supposed to figure out what they were thinking?

"Shouldn't be long," the geezer said.

Something in his tone set Lucie's teeth clattering. She cocked her head, studying his body language, the emotionless stare of a man who'd been working homicide too long.

Lucie strode to the door, swung it open, and peeped outside. No Willie. Okay. She wouldn't panic. She met her best friend's eyes as Ro walked toward her. The younger detective checked out Ro's recently acquired ample bottom.

"Hey!" Lucie grabbed both men's attention, jabbing two fingers at her eyes. "Eyes up. Do you even know who she is?"

And, dear God, what was she doing? For years Joey had used that "Do you know who I am?" line on people.

Before today, Lucie hated it. After all, wasn't the legend of Joe Rizzo the thing she'd been running from her entire life?

"Luce," Ro said, "call Joey. Tell him where I am."

"Don't you worry. We'll be down there." She exchanged a look with the geezer. "Waiting for you to come out."

"Thanks, Luce. I love you."

"I love you too. But, for the love of God, don't say anything. Not one thing until Willie gets there."

"THIS I DIDN'T SEE COMING," DAD SAID.

He sat back on the wooden bench in the police station lobby and crossed his arms, his gaze following Lucie as she paced. She reached the entrance, swiveled, and started another lap. How long did they intend to keep Ro in there?

"Me neither, Dad."

Joey, to his credit, had been insanely calm, sitting on that same bench, tapping his sneaker-clad foot, playing on his phone, and generally keeping his mouth shut. A miracle in itself. Now he looked over at their father. "What?"

"For once I'm the one out here." Dad swung his thumb. "Usually, I'm the guy back there."

Really? He was going there? Lucie shook her head and completed another lap. On the turn, she tossed a glance at the receptionist sitting behind the glass partition separating the small lobby from the administrative area.

As police stations went, this one wasn't so bad. More modern with tiled floors and gray walls that, based on the lack of bruising, must have been recently painted.

And it didn't stink of stale, closed-in air. Another plus.

"Luce," Joey said, "is this about those stupid dog outfits?"

Her brother. The idiot.

"First of all, they're not stupid. Ro works hard—extremely hard—on her designs. Sometimes it takes her months to get one perfect. Someone stealing them is...hurtful. It's her work. She's proud of it."

"But are they worth this?" Her brother glanced at the receptionist typing away on her computer.

Rather than talk from across the room, Lucie halted in front Joey and dipped her head close to his ear. "I think the tweet must have started this."

"What tweet?"

He didn't know about the infamous tweet. Not surprising, considering the way he and Ro hightailed it out of mom's last night. Being the horndogs they were, Lucie didn't expect they did much catching up overnight. Outside of the dirty talk Ro thought it was funny to tell Lucie they excelled at.

Blech.

Lucie shoved it from her mind. Hard. "Ro had a bad day yesterday, what with you acting like an ass." Before he could mouth off, she held up her hand. "Don't say it. We're talking about Ro, who went a little cuckoo. When she was cruising Twitter, she saw one of her designs in Buzzy's feed and—"

"Crap."

Yep. "She, uh, *responded.*"

Joey ran both hands through his thick dark hair then hunched over, resting his elbows on his knees. "Do I want to know what she said?"

"Ro called her a thieving bitch. Actually, she said *beyotch.*"

"Ah, hell."

Joey stood and shoved his phone in the back pocket of his jeans before folding his arms. "They dragged her down here for *that*? Are you kidding me? Last I heard, there wasn't a law against telling the truth. Buzzy is—"

"Was."

"*Was* a thieving bitch."

Dad circled a hand. "I keep telling the boys that twitting is bad news."

Somehow Lucie couldn't picture a bunch of mob guys sitting around Petey's making up funny hashtags.

Joey sighed. "It's *tweeting.* Not twitting."

"Eh." Dad waved him off. "It's nothing but trouble, that's what it is."

For once, Lucie agreed with her father.

A door slammed from inside somewhere and Joey

angled back, his face showing signs of relief that maybe Ro might soon join them. But, nope. Just a uniformed cop talking to the receptionist.

"It's been over an hour," Joey said.

"Ninety minutes actually."

And counting. Which meant that any second now either Joey or Dad would suggest she call Tim. No matter how many times she told her family she wouldn't involve Tim in their legal affairs, it never quite sank in.

"Call Tim," Joey said. "See if he can tell you anything."

There it was. "Joey, please. You know I can't."

"You *won't*. Big difference."

"That is *not* fair. If I thought he could help, I'd call him. This isn't even his precinct. And he's not homicide. He probably knows as much as we do."

"Yeah, but you could ask."

"It's not right to put him in that position."

Dad held up his hands. "I agree with your brother."

As if that were late-breaking news. "Well, Dad, I'm not asking Tim to risk his job by leaking information. If you want to have one of your cronies do that, fine, but I won't."

On cue, Lucie's phone rang. Tim's ringtone. She slid the phone out of her pocket, grabbed her coat from the arm of the bench, and headed for the doors.

"Where you going?" Dad wanted to know.

"This is Tim. His ears are probably on fire."

"Luce," Joey called. "Please, just talk to him."

Oh, snap. When he asked like that, all pleading and nice, how could she refuse?

Complications. Serious complications. All thanks to her last name and the ramifications that came with it.

On the third ring, she poked at the screen. "Hey," she said into the phone.

She pushed through the station door and was hit with an icy blast of wind that should have sliced her in half. Damned lake wind. A stark reminder that Lucie hadn't had a vacation in two years. After this, she wanted one. With Tim. Somewhere warm where they could sit around and drink silly frozen cocktails all day.

"Hi. Where are you?"

A man carrying a briefcase strode toward her and she sidestepped to avoid smacking into him. Once he was gone, she hunched her shoulders and wedged herself between the doorway and the barely two feet of alcove wall that blocked the wind. Moments like these, she blessed the gods that had made her small enough to fit into confined spaces.

"I'm at the police station."

"They brought you downtown?"

"Actually, surprise, surprise, they didn't come looking for *me*."

"Come again?"

"As we expected, two detectives showed up this morning. I was all ready for them, but they wanted Ro."

"Ro?" Judging by Tim's reaction, he didn't know diddly.

"I take it you didn't hear?"

"Not a peep. It's actually impressive how tight they're keeping this. Considering who she was and the media frenzy, the brass doesn't want any leaks. Did they question you? At all?"

"No. They came into the shop, asked for Ro, and brought her down here. She's been in there almost two hours. Is that bad?"

Tim's silence gave her the answer.

"It's always bad when you're quiet."

"Relax. I'm thinking. It's not necessarily bad. They might

have her on ice while they look into a couple things. She has a lawyer, right?"

"Of course. Willie."

Tim had the nerve to laugh. Part of Lucie couldn't blame him. At this point, the Rizzo bunch should have a dedicated phone line to Willie Clay, defense attorney extraordinaire. Still, Ro didn't deserve to be sitting in some crummy interrogation room being grilled.

"Laughing? Really?"

"You're right. I'm sorry. You guys keep Willie hopping."

"Dad had him on alert at Petey's in case the cops showed up for me. I swear that man could buy a vacation home or two with the fees he collects from my family."

Another blast of wind whipped and she burrowed further into the alcove.

"Tim?"

"Yeah?"

"I'm worried. I mean, she sent out that damned tweet. They probably went straight to Buzzy's social media accounts looking for haters and found Ro. She basically put herself on a silver platter."

"Okay, calm down."

"I hate when people tell me to calm down."

"I'm doing it anyway. Don't get ahead of yourself. This is a murder investigation. They'll work through all the possibilities and start eliminating people. Yeah, it's unfortunate about the tweet, but they'll talk to her, figure out that she was just being Ro, and they'll let her go. Don't make yourself crazy. Believe me. This is standard procedure."

Lucie drew a breath. Standard procedure. Yes. She'd go with that. A woman had lost her life. Had it been one of Lucie's loved ones, she'd expect detectives to question the entire city.

"Wait," she said. "The security system. When Ro and I were at Buzzy's, she was showing us how she could pull up live video on her tablet. At any time, she could log on and see what was happening at the house. If the system was activated, they'd have everything on video."

"Let me pass that along. See what pops."

How much did she adore Tim O'Brien? Cool and unruffled, the man knew how to talk her down. To get her off the highest of ledges. These past few months with him had been heaven. Literally. If they argued, it lasted 3.5 seconds and then it was done. No lingering bitterness, no prolonged silent treatment like Joey and Ro. No drama. Zero.

"Thank you," Lucie said.

"You're welcome. Honestly, don't get worked up. With the media hype on this, I think everyone is a suspect right now. And thank *you*."

"For what?"

"Respecting the boundaries. You didn't ask me to snoop around."

"Don't give me too much credit. I almost caved to pressure. I'm sitting here with Joey and Dad, after all. It came up, but I told them to forget it. Because, guess what, big guy?"

"What?"

"I happen to love you and don't want you put in an uncomfortable place because of my last name."

"Got it," Tim said to someone on the other end. "I'm on it, boss. Luce? I gotta run. Call me when Ro is done. Keep me updated."

"I will."

5
—————

LUCIE WALKED BACK INTO THE POLICE STATION AND FOUND THE guy with the briefcase sitting opposite Joey and Dad. He looked over at her and nodded a greeting. She did the same. Even on a really hard day common courtesy never hurt.

From her coat pocket, Lucie's phone *tinkled* the arrival of a text.

Joey waved her to his spot on the bench. "Who's that? Tim? Did you talk to him? What'd he say?"

Yeesh with the rapid-fire questions. "Hold on. It's Willie."

She tapped the message envelope and...*wait*.

"Oh, no. No. No. *No*."

Okay. So maybe that last no got a little loud. She looked around, found the owl-eyed receptionist staring at her and the guy on the bench shaking his head.

Joey sidled up next to her and read the text over her shoulder.

"Are you effing kidding me?" His voice boomed in the confined area and Lucie winced.

Dad's head snapped up. "What happened?"

"Unbelievable!" Joey flung a hand out. "The dumbasses are *arresting* her."

Talk about getting loud. "Sssh," Lucie said. "Keep it down, will you?"

"Both of you relax. It's a misunderstanding that's all."

It'd better be. This was nuts. Ro? Arrested for murder. Ridiculous. This was Lucie's BFF, the woman who'd protected her all through school, the one who'd listened and consoled her every time a boy broke her heart. The one who'd helped her launch Coco Barknell.

"You bet your life it's a misunderstanding," Lucie said. "Do these detectives have nothing better to do than harass honest citizens? The real killer is out there and they're wasting time with Ro. Give me a break."

"This is news to you?" Dad asked, his voice thick with sarcasm. "After all I've been through with the legal system? Now you know how I felt."

Oh, please. Totally different scenario. Considering what her father did for a living. Why did every damned thing revolve around Dad and his legal issues?

"This is bullshit," Joey said.

The receptionist stood and knocked on the glass partition. "Folks, you need to pipe down or we'll ask you to leave."

Ha! Ask them to leave? As if *they* were the issue?

Nice.

Try.

Lucie swung and faced the woman. "I'm not going anywhere until I get some answers. You people have just locked up an innocent woman. It's *insane!*"

Dad, apparently the reasonable one—a first for sure—patted the air. "Calm down." He stood, holding up his phone. "Let me get Willie. He'll explain all this."

"You do that," Lucie said.

The interior door opened and two uniformed cops stepped out. "Everything all right out here?"

"Everything is most certainly *not* all right." Holy cow, Lucie must have been channeling Ro.

"What's the problem?" the taller cop asked.

At least a foot shorter than the cop, Lucie screwed up her courage and puffed out her chest. "Two detectives have just arrested my friend. I'd like to know why."

"I'm sure you would, but you need to keep your voice down. We're not gonna have this out here."

If it got Ro out of this mess, they'd have it wherever Lucie said they'd have it. "I want to see Roseanne Buccarelli. Right now."

"She's being processed. No visitors. Leave your number and I'll have her lawyer call you."

"I'm sure," Lucie snapped. Was she being nasty? Yes. Absolutely. But...Ro? In jail? If it wasn't so dumb, it would be comical.

Stop. She needed to get hold of her emotions. Another switch. What was going on around here today with everyone acting out of character? Normally, she was the sane one. *Deep breath, Luce. Deep breath.*

"Miss," the other cop said.

She opened her eyes just as he lightly touched her arm. She peered up at his kind eyes and immediately knew he was one of the good ones. A man who'd become a cop to serve. To help people. Maybe he could help her.

"Whoa," Joey said. "Hands off my sister."

What? She swung her head in his direction and nearly reared back at the carved tightness in his cheeks. The pressed lips. Her brother, if they didn't do something, was about to blow. In truth, his rage probably had nothing to do with this cop barely—*barely*—touching her and everything to do with Ro being locked up.

Whatever the reason, it wasn't good. She knew her brother. For years she'd watched him operate. When it came to a hair trigger, Joey had been cursed. He took hair triggers to another level. A double hair trigger. Maybe even a triple.

Cop number one nudged in closer, getting in Joey's space. "You don't tell us what to do. *We* tell you what to do. Now leave."

Oh, boy.

"You—" Dad poked his finger at Joey, "—calm down. Right now. Don't even think about busting this place up."

"Ray," cop number two said, "I've got this."

Except Joey inched closer, and with him came an electric buzz that sent the energy in the room crackling. "Get away from my father before I kick your ass."

Ohmygod. "Joey! Stop it."

The cop snorted. "You think you're gonna kick my ass. That's it. Up against the wall."

Could there be anything worse than a bunch of high-strung alphas in a confined space? Enough already. Lucie wedged herself between Joey and the jerky cop and shoved. Unfortunately, at 6'5", her brother was basically a human mountain and didn't budge. Lucie dug her heels in and threw all her weight forward. Pushing, pushing, pushing. Her sneakers squeaked against the tile and...*grrrr*...began to slip.

Damn it.

Joey grabbed her by the arms, picked her up—*whoopsie*—and set her beside him.

Well, that was a bust.

The cop inched closer and Lucie inserted herself into

the fray again, throwing her elbows to separate the two men. Damned Joey. He'd get them all arrested.

Cop number two stepped in, pointed at Lucie and Joey. "I want you two over there."

"Bullshit," cop one said. "I'm arresting him."

First Ro, now Joey. For the love of God.

"On what charge?" Joey said.

"Resisting arrest. I told you to put your hands on that wall."

Cop one reached up...and shoved Joey, sending him back a step. *That'll do it.* A sudden pained look crossed cop number two's face.

Joey shoved back and Lucie rushed in to break it up. She plowed into cop one, and once again the petite one was overmatched. She bounced off him and flew backward, sticking her hands out behind her to break her fall. She hit the tile, her wrists taking the brunt of it before her rear got in on the act. Pain shot straight up her arms clear to her shoulders. Dang, that hurt.

And Joey saw red. Well, first he saw his sister flat on her ass and then he saw red.

On his best day, her brother set an example for idiots everywhere. She'd be the first to tell him that. Above all that moronic behavior, though, was a man fiercely loyal and protective of his loved ones. In his mind, that cop had just put her on the floor.

So what did he do? He shoved the jerky cop again. Of course he did. Testosterone must have flooded the jerky cop because he shoved back. The nice cop got between them. Dad hollered at everyone to knock it off, because he was on parole and couldn't get in the middle of the whole thing.

Lucie stood stunned. Completely gobsmacked at the sight of her brother being manhandled by two Chicago cops. Something sparked inside her. Idiot or not, she loved Joey and it was two against one.

And those were never good odds. Next to her, Dad made a move to step in. No. He couldn't do that. They'd lock him up, and her mother would face the humiliation of having a jailbird husband all over again.

So Lucie did the only thing she could.

She leaped, landing on the jerky cop's back, wrapping her arms around his shoulders, and hanging on as he swung around trying to buck her off. If she could hold on long enough, he'd step back from Joey and not do some sort of crazy body flip on her. Hopefully. One could never tell in a situation like this.

Please.

All she needed was to distract him long enough for the nice cop to get control of the situation.

"What the hell?" the jerky cop yelled.

"He's my brother," Lucie said, "I'm not letting you hurt him."

"Get off me. Right now."

The interior door flew open and four, no, five more cops streamed out. Their shouts filled the small lobby and ricocheted off the walls. Two of them headed toward Lucie and the other three to Joey, who was still trying to get around the nice cop to kick the jerk cop's ass.

"Police brutality," someone yelled. Lucie swiveled her head to see the guy with the briefcase taping the whole thing.

Just got worse.

LUCIE'S REAR HURT.

She sat on the metal bench inside the temporary holding cell, really just a giant cage, inside the administrative area of the police station. In the bullpen, half a dozen cops went about their business, answering ringing phones and snickering at the Rizzo kids locked up like animals.

Another day in paradise.

At least Dad had managed to stay out of the melee while Lucie and Joey were fitted with handcuffs.

Arrested. Unbelievable. This made two trips to the clink for Lucie. Technically, the first time didn't count because she'd been framed. It sounded lame, without a doubt, but her sanity depended on that line of thinking. She'd spent her entire adult life trying to be the good one in the family. Honest, hardworking, make-her-own-way Lucie.

Except, she'd now been arrested more times than Joey. Joey, the bookie, before today, had never been arrested.

Across from Lucie, Ro slid off her shoes and leaned on one of the cell's support poles. She swung her head to the cage beside them—the men's cage—where Joey sulked on his own bench.

"Well, I'll say this, you're the family that stays together. Just lovely."

"Shut it, Roseanne," he said.

Good thing male and female prisoners needed to be separated. Between the mutinous look on Ro's face and her miserable mood, she might have scratched Joey's eyes out. Their truce had been short-lived.

In the bullpen, one of the cops looked over at them and laughed. *Great. Let's throw gas on this fire.*

Lucie rose from her seat and walked to the wired-mesh wall separating the two cells. "Let's not talk. Okay? Willie is working on bond for Joey and me. Then we'll deal with getting Ro out."

Ro let out a grunt. "I swear, I don't know how you two got into this mess. All you had to do was get me a lawyer and you wind up right here with me."

"*Well*," Joey's voice boomed, "maybe you shouldn't have sent that damned tweet and none of us would be here."

Lucie whirled on him. "Joey!"

Too late. Ro smacked the wired mesh and Lucie winced. That had to hurt.

"You're an animal, Joey. Why I ever got mixed up with you is beyond me. Every place we go, you're looking for a fight. I'm done. I can't take it anymore."

"Pipe down in there," one of the cops yelled.

"Oh, pipe down yourself," Ro hollered back.

Now that was funny. Lucie couldn't help laughing. Maybe it was her own weird form of stress relief. All she knew was that the day had been straight out of hell.

"Officer," Lucie said, "take my advice. Don't engage them. It'll only get worse. I find if I ignore it, they'll stop."

"Screw you, Luce," Joey said.

Lucie jerked her thumb at Joey. "Case in point. If I don't respond, he'll leave me alone. Exactly what I want."

"What *I* want," the cop said, "is for all of you to shut the hell up." He spun his chair back to address the room at large. "Anyone have word on transport for this bunch?"

One of the other cops scooped up his desk phone. "Nothing yet. We're stuck with them."

TIM STRODE THROUGH THE FRONT DOOR OF THE STATION, badged the receptionist, and waited for her to buzz Sergeant Kristoff, a guy Tim had been through the academy with.

Thankfully, Kristoff wasn't involved in whatever screwed

up assaulting-an-officer scenario Lucie and Joey had going here, but he'd been one of the cops to break the whole thing up.

As soon as Lucie's father had called, Tim punched up Kristoff for the full story on how the love of his life wound up in a holding cell.

The Rizzo bunch. Never a dull moment.

If Lucie kept this up, Tim's stomach would disintegrate. Not to mention the career implications of having a girlfriend with a tendency to get locked up. This nonsense had to stop.

The interior door swung open and Kristoff waved him in.

After shaking hands, Kristoff smacked Tim on the back. "Do us a favor and get them out of here. My man, you got your hands full with this girl."

If Tim had it in him, he'd have laughed. As it stood now, none of it amused him. "You have no idea. Any chance I can get them out with a citation?"

Each of them getting a fine would be the simplest thing for the PD—and Lucie and Joey. The Rizzo name drew attention. Ro suddenly being arrested for murder and being the girlfriend of Joe Rizzo Junior? Forget it. For the media, it would be a hit of acid.

"Brass is behind closed doors now talking about it. This thing is ripe with problems." He held up his thumb. "We got Joe Rizzo's kids. You know the curiosity that creates." His index finger went next. "Then we got a hot-headed cop who just came off administrative leave." His middle finger went next. "Add in the video and it's a PR cluster."

Tim stopped walking. "Video? What video?"

"Ambulance chaser in the lobby when it went down. He's already screaming about police brutality. I'm guessing the brass'll want this whole thing to go away. Any help on your end would, I'm sure, be appreciated."

Meaning, get Lucie and Joey to shut up about this whole episode and they might be able to walk free. Could they all get that lucky?

Tim nodded. "I'll take care of it."

They walked down the short hallway to the bullpen. As soon as Tim entered, he spotted the two mesh cages in the back of the room. Seeing Lucie in that cage tore something inside him.

Cluster.

Ro spotted him first and wagged a finger. "Don't be mad at Lucie, O'Hottie. It's not *her* fault Joey can't control himself."

"O'Hottie?" Kristoff said. "That's beautiful."

Tim ignored him. Any reaction would bring a shitstorm of heckles from the rest of the room. It would probably happen anyway, but Tim wasn't about to help the process along. Bad enough he'd have to deal with the speculation about his relationship with the Rizzos.

Kristoff left Tim at the cage and disappeared behind a door to the right.

"Technically," Lucie said, "it's my fault. I jumped on the guy's back. I was afraid Joey would get hurt, and, well, you know how I am. I can't let that happen."

As much as he hated sighing, Tim let out the mother of all sighs. *She's killing me.*

Why did she have to be so damn cute?

Joey walked to the adjoining mesh wall of the holding cell. "*I* can't control myself? You broads are nuts. We wouldn't be locked up if it weren't for you two."

"And it starts again," one of the cops announced over the ringing phones. "Any word on that transport?

Anything? I'll drive them myself. Where are the keys to the van?"

Kristoff emerged again and waved at the cop. "Knock it off, Conklin,"

He pointed to Lucie, then to Joey. "You two. We're releasing you with a citation."

Lucie—all big eyes and wonder—slid her gaze to Tim, then back to Kristoff. "Really?"

Kristoff opened the cell door, but Lucie spun back to Ro, who stood there, her pretty face rapidly losing color. Certain things Tim couldn't fathom. Roseanne standing in front of him in terror would be one of them. Lucie threw her arms around her and held on.

"You'll be okay," she said. "I promise. We'll get you out of here. Willie is good. You know that."

Ro squeezed her eyes closed and Tim had to look away. Had to. Ro was usually the one helping Lucie out of these jams. He wasn't sure if either of them knew what to do with the situation reversed.

He himself felt...stuck. His love for Lucie dictated he should do something, anything, to protect her from the heartbreak of her closest friend being charged with murder. That love sat in direct opposition to his job. And his boss, knowing his involvement with Lucie, had obviously boxed him out. Tim hadn't even known they were questioning Ro. Not a scrap of information thrown his way. Did it bug him?

Sure did.

It stunk to admit it, but he'd spent over ten years building a career, being promoted to detective and enjoying a reputation based on the trust of his superiors. Now?

No intel. Nothing.

At least until Tim called Kristoff.

Hard not to resent the big freeze-out. All because Lucie and her crazy family couldn't stay out of trouble.

"Ladies," Kristoff said, "move it along."

Lucie leaped back and squeezed Ro's arms. "I've got you. Don't worry."

Then she turned and met Tim's eye, that fierce determination he adored about her firmly in place.

Before Kristoff opened Joey's cell, Ro walked to the adjoining wall and murmured something. Whatever it was, it brought a sad smile to Joey's face.

"I know," he said, lifting his hand and pressing it against the wall. "I'll take care of it. We'll have you out by morning."

"Thank you," Ro said. "I love you."

"Love you too. Just don't get crazy in here."

"Too late for that," one of the cops yelled.

Alright, enough from the peanut gallery. Tim turned and shot him a look. The guy shrugged. "This chick is crazy."

"All of you," Kristoff said, "cut the crap. Right now."

What the brass wanted to avoid was any scrutiny—from wherever— of this incident. Particularly with the ambulance chaser crying brutality.

Something told Tim he hadn't heard the last of that video, but he couldn't deal with it now. One thing at a time.

Where Lucie was concerned, that wasn't always easy.

Kristoff processed Joey and Lucie while Tim waited near the back door of the station, where the brass decided it would be in everyone's best interest if Lucie and Joey exited. Reporters swarmed the front, but with the gate around the back, couldn't get to that door.

So Tim waited, returning calls regarding a robbery he'd handled that morning. They had a lead on a suspect, and he needed to wrap up here and hit the pavement. First things first.

Joey and Lucie swung around the corner, the two of them droopy-eyed, pale, and more worn than Tim had ever seen. Throw in the wrinkled clothes and they'd had a day.

"You both okay?"

Joey nodded and Lucie glanced back down the hallway to the bullpen. And presumably her closest friend.

She paused for a solid ten seconds, raised her hands then, as if the weight of the world had driven them down, let them drop. "I can't go. How do we just...leave her here?"

That right there, that fierce loyalty—no matter what—was the thing that made Lucie Rizzo the love of Tim's life. The thing that kept him coming back when the chaos of her life had him chasing his tail. And, even now, when his lieutenant had by-passed him and asked a few of his fellow detectives to help with the Buzzy Sneider murder, Tim found it impossible to abandon Lucie. She might kill him before he reached forty, but if he played it right, she'd be by his side when he died.

"Luce," he said, "I promise you, they'll take care of her. Everything will be by the book. What the brass doesn't want is any additional attention about Buzzy's case. And they really don't want hype about the three of you being locked up together."

"Because we're Rizzos?"

No way to deny it. "Yes. This case is already tearing up the Chicago airwaves. We don't need to throw Ro's connection to Joe Rizzo Senior into it."

A cop strode by, shifting a gaze at Tim. By nature, cops were nosey people. At least the ones Tim knew. He didn't consider it a bad thing if it kept people safe.

Then again, he didn't need an audience right now. He snagged Lucie's coat from her and held it open. "Let's move this outside"

She shoved her arms through, her hands automatically moving to the buttons while he straightened her collar the way she liked it. "Thank you. I know you got us out of there."

"I didn't do much, Luce."

"You sped things up, though. I'm sorry if we embarrassed you."

"Would I prefer it didn't happen? Yeah, but that's because I don't want you dealing with it. It's not about me. I'm a big boy."

"I keep telling her that," Joey said.

For the most part, Tim was entertained by Joey. Bookmaking aside, he and Tim were of the same mind about plenty of things. Taking care of their loved ones sat at the top of the list. On this topic? Solidly in the same camp.

Lucie stood on tip-toes and kissed his cheek. Seriously, how cute was she?

"You're a good man, Tim O'Brien."

"Blah, blah," Joey said. "Can we save this lovey-dovey crap for later and talk about Ro?"

"You're such a jerk."

Cripes. Tim held his hands up. "Outside."

They strode through the doors to the back walkway and hunched against the wind in front of an unmarked department vehicle.

"I guess," Lucie said, "she'll be arraigned soon."

Sad, the familiarity with the legal system. Tim nodded. "She'll have a hearing and they'll talk bond."

"When is that?"

"It has to be within 48 hours," Joey said.

Lucie shot him a surprised look.

"When Dad got arrested, I wanted to know how long it would take to get him bailed out. I did research."

"He's right. Here's the bad news. Bond court starts at 1:00. Monday through Friday."

Lucie's eyebrows rose. "But it's five now."

"Which means..."

"Oh my God. She's going to be in jail overnight. Just stop it!"

What did she think? The criminal justice system would allow a murder suspect to waltz out of custody. *Oh, you can go now. Come back tomorrow.*

"Honey, it's a homicide. They're not about to let her walk out."

"But she's *innocent.*"

Okay. His girl was too hyped up to discuss the finer points of the judicial system. And Tim wasn't about to get into an argument behind the PD.

"Luce," Joey said, "don't get worked up. We're at step one in a fifty-step process. I'll talk to Willie, see what they've got on her that was enough to get her locked up." He looked at Tim. "I mean, it has to be more than that damned tweet."

"They've got something. Before you ask, I don't know what it is. With the media frenzy, they're keeping details on lockdown."

Joey waved a hand. "I'll work it from my end. Dad has someone he can reach out to."

Moments like this, Tim pretended he was deaf. Made life—and his stress level—more tolerable. "I didn't just hear that."

Lucie nodded. "I'll go through all of Ro's emails and social media accounts. See if there's anything crazy in there. She threatens to kill people twelve times a day. It doesn't mean she'll actually do it."

Joey shook his head and blew out a burst of air.

Lucie, hands still shoved in her coat pockets, hunched her shoulders. "What?"

"Nothing. The whole damned thing. She's locked up and it's flipping cold out here. I told her I'd go see her folks and update them."

"I'm coming with you," Lucie said.

"Good. That'll help. You know her mother with the drama."

Two drama queens in one family? God bless Roseanne's father.

Tim set a hand on Lucie's shoulder. "I have to go. I'm working a case. Call me if you need something, but I'll probably be late. You okay?"

"I'm good. Thank you."

Tim smiled and—eh, the hell with it—dipped his head and kissed her. The nosey cops inside would have a field day, but he loved this woman and, sooner or later, he'd have to face the repercussions. Whatever they might be.

A Chicago detective and the daughter of a notorious mob boss. Talk about a media frenzy.

"Well," Lucie said. "That stunk."

She sat in the passenger side of Joey's SUV, staring at the home she'd spent so much of her teenaged years in. Sleepovers, dinners, birthday parties, all of it hosted by Ro's parents. Well, her mother really. If Ro was Queen of all Things Fabulous, she'd learned every bit of it from her mom.

Who'd spent the last twenty minutes bawling her eyes out in her bedroom, too sick to even come out and talk to Joey and Lucie. So they'd spent those twenty minutes sharing everything they knew with Mr. Buccarelli and promising to keep him updated.

"You know," Joey said, "this nonsense is wearing me out. Between Dad, you, and now Ro, how is it I've turned into the good one?"

"Go figure."

At that, they both laughed. One of those *isn't-this-ironic* snorting laughs.

Joey vacated a no-parking zone. In this neighborhood, an unspoken agreement existed between residents and law enforcement. As long as you weren't blocking a fire hydrant and didn't intend to stay long, you were safe in a no-parking zone.

Lucie still didn't understand the logic, but that was Franklin.

"Can you run me by the office? I want to look at Ro's emails."

"Yeah. We're going there anyway. Making a stop first."

"What stop?"

"At my place."

"Why?"

"When we were talking with your boyfriend about what the cops had on Ro, I had a thought."

Lucie faced her brother. "You didn't want to talk in front of Tim, did you?"

"I like him, but he's a cop and I don't know how the hell to deal with that."

"Welcome to my world." She shook it off. "What weren't you saying?"

"I was thinking about Ro threatening to kill people all the time. Do you remember her saying anything like that about this witch Buzzy?" He held a hand up. "God rest her soul."

"Please. At least ten times a day."

"In the office?"

"Yes. Why?"

Joey kept his eyes on the road, but ran his hand over his mouth, back and forth, back and forth, a habit he'd picked up from their dad when mentally working through something.

"Joey?"

"I never told you this, but when Dad went away, I bought a bug detector. Dad knew Petey's was bugged. Still is. He wanted me to make sure the house was clean. So, you know, Mom would have her privacy. I'd check the house a few times a week. I even found a couple of the little bastards and ripped them out. After the first three times, the government gave up. Guess they figured we were boring and it wasn't worth the effort. Or the cost of replacement."

Lucie had never known this and the constantly simmering resentment that came with being the daughter of a mobster spiked to a boil. Her father was free to make his own choices, but those choices reflected on his wife and children. All this time, they'd been subjected to his bad decisions and now this? Being spied on in their own home?

Disgusting.

"I..." She stopped, closed her mouth, and stared out the windshield at a starlit sky.

"What? I know you have something to say about it. I'm not gonna get lucky enough on this truly suckfest of a day to have you not rail about Dad's lifestyle."

"Actually, no. It's not your fault. Thank you for not telling me. I think that would have freaked me out. That they were listening."

"Well, Luce, I hate to tell you, but I think they're listening all right. Just not in the house."

"YOU THINK OUR OFFICE IS *BUGGED*?"

Lucie rested her head back, staring straight ahead at the cars littering Franklin Avenue. Mrs. DeSantis had stopped right in the middle to carry on a conversation with someone driving a Buick.

Joey honked to let them know it was time to break it up, and Mrs. D. waved before moving on. "I don't know," he said. "We'll find out."

Thinking on it, her office being monitored made sense. Every day Dad wandered down from Petey's to, as he put it, check on them. With all those trips, the feds might think her father conducted business out of her shop.

That alone fried her.

Joey swung a left, heading to his place, the home still owned by Lucie's ex, Frankie. She hated going there. As much as she loved Tim, the way things ended with Frankie bothered her. They had history together, years of loving each other and family friendships to boot. Now he was gone. Out of her life with zero communication. Somehow, it didn't seem right.

"The feds are still watching Petey's," Joey said.

"And it's not a stretch that they might think he's using Coco Barknell for business dealings."

Which, to her father's credit, he'd never done. He'd respected her wishes to keep her business legitimate.

Still, the feds wouldn't know that. Unless they planted listening devices.

Lucie let out a rueful laugh. All that BS about working hard and rising above the mob princess moniker had gotten her was a business under surveillance.

Horror renewed, Lucie ticked back over the last few days. "Since this whole thing with Buzzy stealing the designs started, Ro has threatened to kill her twelve different ways and...oh, no."

"Luce?"

She ran her fingers into her hair and tugged, allowing the pain to penetrate and bring her emotions back in line. "Just yesterday Ro said she wanted to wrap her fingers around Buzzy's scrawny neck. And then hours later the woman was found asphyxiated. If our office is bugged..."

"That's what the cops have on her."

"Yes."

"We're screwed."

"WELL, WELL, WELL."

Dead center between Ro and Lucie's desks, Joey stood on a step stool, shoving one of the drop-ceiling panels aside. He poked his head into the square, shining the flashlight one direction then the other.

"Did you find something?"

"I sure did."

He reached into the ceiling and came out with a tiny black device no bigger than a postage stamp. Hopping down from the stool, he dropped the bug on the tile. The tiny smack of plastic shouldn't have bothered her. Shouldn't have sounded like her world crashing in. Shouldn't have meant her bestie under arrest over conversations had in the so-called privacy of this office.

"Party is over, boys." Joey lifted his giant foot, stomped on the bug, and ground it into the tile. "One down. There might be more."

Still holding the walkie-talkie lookalike detector, Joey continued his exploration of the office with Lucie on his heels. Knowing the feds could be listening, they moved silently. They walked the short hallway to the break room, where Ro had set up a table, chairs and a reading nook. As if they'd read at work. But the overstuffed chairs with cushions deep enough to nap in were a nice touch. Particularly since Tim had gotten a little frisky after work two weeks ago and the two of them...well...they'd broken those chairs in right.

Just thinking about it sent heat to her cheeks. And other places. Because sex with Tim... All that solid muscle that wasn't too cut, but just enough to let everyone know he spent time in the gym? Outstanding. Every time. No matter if they were in a hurry or taking their time. Her cravings for him, like a streaming buzz under her skin, never ended.

Dear God, please don't let there be a bug in here.

Yikes-a-roo. She and her cop boyfriend may have given the feds an X-rated show. Audio porn. So much for Tim thinking he'd done a crack job of balancing his career and his relationship with the mob princess.

Nausea whirled and Lucie ran her palm up her forehead. Tim didn't deserve this. She didn't deserve *him*. Not with the mess of baggage she brought.

The detector beeped and Joey moved left. Toward the reading nook.

"Oh, no," Lucie said.

That sickness whipped at her now and she set her hand over her mouth.

Joey moved closer to the chairs and, *beep-beep, beep-beep-beep*, the damned detector started going haywire.

"There's another one," she said.

"Yep."

Joey stopped in front of the first chair, the one where Tim had blessed her with a mighty orgasm. *Beep-beep-beep-beep-beep*. Apparently, she hadn't been the only thing beeping that night.

Lawdy.

"Ha!" Joey said. "They put one in the cushion."

Gulp.

Oh, those bastards. Flaming heat rose to her cheeks and she pressed her icy fingers against them while Joey set the detector on the arm of the chair, unzipped the cushion cover, and rummaged around. Finally, he snatched the filthy devil free.

Lucie shook her head. Maybe, the bugs hadn't been there long. Maybe...

"Oh, God." She might throw up. Right on that damned cushion. She waggled her hand at Joey. "Give me that thing."

He handed the bug off and she marched to the supply closet Ro had been organizing earlier that day, the supplies still scattered on the floor. In the corner sat a toolbox left by the previous owners. Ro wanted to throw it out because it was old and a little rusty, but Lucie liked the nostalgia of keeping something that belonged to the Carluccis. They had, after all, outfitted her with her first pair of shoes.

She opened the toolbox, the hinges squeaking as she lifted the lid and—there—right on top sat the hammer.

Hefting the hammer, she nodded. The people on the other end of this damned listening device had heard her and Tim making love. Saying...*things*. Having fun in what should have been a private moment.

A private moment that was probably now fodder for some voyeuristic federal agents. And if the feds were working in conjunction with Chicago PD and knew Tim was a detective the poor guy would never live it down.

By law, if a conversation wasn't criminal-related, authorities weren't allowed to listen. But who knew if someone had gotten their kicks by eavesdropping?

Smash! Lucie pummeled the tiny square device. Just beat that sucker to a fast and painful death.

"Take that. Jerks!"

Behind her came a slow clap. *Clap, clap, clap.*

Joey. Being a smartass, no doubt.

She swung back and shook the hammer at him. "Not one word or I swear, I will beat you with this hammer."

"Hey, I'm proud of you. Usually by now you're screaming about it being Dad's fault."

"They bugged my shop. Do you think if my last name wasn't Rizzo they would have done that?"

"Joe Rizzo comes here every day—it doesn't matter what your last name is. Look at Petey."

That shut her up. Stopped her cold. For once, her heritage didn't matter. All that mattered was her link to Joe Rizzo, mob boss. And now Ro was suspected of murder and that bug probably helped to build a case against her.

Lucie tossed the hammer back into the toolbox. "We should tell Willie about these bugs. Maybe he can do his magic and get any recordings thrown out. They're has to be some obscure reason they could be considered unconstitutional."

"I'll call him. Let's finish sweeping first. Make sure we got everything."

Did it matter? The damage had already been done. On several fronts.

———

THE FOLLOWING MORNING, AFTER A STOMACH-CHURNING night of phone tag with Tim, Lucie stood in front of Bergman's, a total throwback of a Jewish deli on the north side of Chicago that served pickles straight out of giant barrels and sandwiches thick as bricks. The homemade bagels had been a mainstay during her banking days.

Today, with Tim staring down at her, his sucked in cheeks and puckered mouth a bizarre mix of disbelief and anger over the audio porn news, she might not even make it inside.

He had never been ashamed of his relationship with her. If people knew, they knew. But his career was important to him and Lucie didn't want him suffering because of her. At her request, they'd spent these last months navigating the fine line between flaunting their relationship and keeping it on the down low.

"I'm sorry," she said. "I didn't know."

"Obviously." He gritted his teeth and muttered an F-bomb. "A bug. I should have anticipated that."

"We all should have. Anyway, I don't know if they heard us or not, but..."

"Yeah. Not good, Luce."

She dipped her head and nodded. "I'm sorry."

"I know you're sorry. But somehow we still wind up in

some kind of Rizzo shit storm. I don't know how this keeps happening."

The irritated tone set her back a step. For the most part, Tim took Lucie's dustups in stride. The man saw all kinds of depravity in his job. Lucie? Small potatoes.

Until now. Now, he seemed...pissed.

Or humiliated.

He let out a long sigh. "Even if they heard us, the feds can't use it. That's not to say the guys at the station won't get wind and crucify me over it."

What had she done to this poor man? "I don't know what to say."

"Say you'll stop with the screwball investigations. This bug thing you couldn't control. The other stuff? Getting into a smack down with cops and getting arrested? I think that could have been avoided."

Before she could fly into her defense, he shook his head. "Forget it. I know what you're gonna say. You were watching out for Joey. I get that. Except, you have no idea how this tears me up. All I want is to protect you, but I'm caught in the middle. And my boss is giving me the deep freeze. Suddenly, I'm not assisting on a big case. Doesn't take a rocket scientist to figure out the brass is afraid I'll tell you sensitive information. If I share anything with you, I could lose my career. No law enforcement agency would touch me if I got fired for sharing information with Joe Rizzo's kid."

A woman cruised by, checking Tim out as she passed, and Lucie gritted her teeth. *Seriously, lady?*

Tim kept his gaze on Lucie. *My man.*

Only, her man just got finished telling her she was creating all sorts of problems for him. Problems he could easily rid himself of. All he'd have to do is...oh no.

She steadied herself, pressing her heels into the ground.

Time to face it. Just ask him straight out and be ready for whatever answer he gave. Even if it devastated her. "Tim, are you dumping me?"

"What? No!"

Phew. "Okay. Wow. You scared me there."

He grabbed her cheeks and kissed her. —right in front of Bergman's!—and Lucie went up on tip-toes, sliding her hands over his shoulders, holding on. Anything to get closer and just enjoy the relief. Suddenly, the thought of life without Tim had become a real possibility. She couldn't lose him. She loved him too much.

But she'd learned the hard way that love didn't always conquer all.

Still, knowing he'd be willing to deal with Rizzo nonsense, said a lot. Such a good man. She backed away from the kiss and met his gaze. "I'm totally in love with you. You know that, right?"

A small smile split his lips. "I know. I love you too. I'm...frustrated. That's all. Are we okay?"

Somehow it should have been her asking that question. "Absolutely."

"Good."

His phone blurted the now familiar ringtone assigned to his boss. Typically, a text was followed by Tim running off to fulfill his civil servant duties.

"Crap," he said. "Home invasion. I'm sorry, Luce."

"It's all right. I have a lot to do before Ro's arraignment anyway. I'll just grab a bagel."

Tim responded to his boss and shoved the phone in his coat pocket. "Call me later and let me know how the arraignment goes."

After a quick kiss, she watched him walk away, his broad form plowing through the morning rush of pedestrians.

Sunlight glinted off his red hair making it look more strawberry blond. Her man.

So different than anyone else she'd been with and, yet, so perfect for her.

Her phone buzzed. Joey disrupting her brief moment of peace. She checked the text and found a link from the local cable news station along with a message.

Welcome to Hollywood.

What the heck did that mean?

She clicked the link and an image of a woman's jean-clad rear filled the screen.

My rear.

"No," she said. "No. No. Noooo."

"Pardon me," a passing woman said.

A guy with a backpack bumped her. "Lady, cripes, you're in the middle of the sidewalk."

Keeping her eyes glued to the phone, she sidestepped. "Sorry. So sorry."

The plight of Catholic Italian girls. Always apologizing.

She shook it off and turned up the volume on her phone. "Police brutality," a man hissed. "Right in front of my eyes."

She knew what this was. *Damn it!*

The image panned wide to show Joey being shoved to the floor while Lucie hung onto the jerky cop's shoulders as he tried to swing her off.

That goofy guy from the police station had released the smack down video to the press.

Lucie looked up, peering through the crowd to where Tim stood at the corner waiting for the light to change. At least she wouldn't have to face him with this latest cluster until this evening. Maybe she'd get lucky and a rampant crime spree would erupt and he'd have to work.

Even for her, this was a banner day. Usually, the Rizzo-related mayhem came in small, sporadic doses.

Today? Two snafus at once.

How much could she expect one hunky Chicago detective to take?

THE COOK COUNTY CRIMINAL COURTS BUILDING, A SCARY stone behemoth known as the old-school courthouse due to its neoclassical architecture, wasn't new territory for the Rizzo family.

Sitting behind the defendant's table in the front row on one of the sturdy oak benches that were murder on the healthiest of backs, Joey leaned forward, talking around Mom to Lucie. "We had a hearing in here once. You were away at school. Bribery charge that time."

"Huh," Dad said from the other side of Lucie. "That was *this* courtroom? I thought it was next door."

"Nope. This one."

Criminal court nostalgia. Excellent.

Dad nudged her with his shoulder. "The charges were dropped. Another case I beat."

Lucie sighed. She must have blocked that particular trial out. Then again, there'd been so many potential cases they all seemed to meld together.

"Willie earned his money that day," Dad said.

Behind them, spectators continued to pour in, folks squeezing into the benches, grabbing every available inch. It wasn't every day a famous reality star suffered an atomic wedgie death. The press wanted in on the action.

A bailiff standing near a door that Lucie assumed led to the judge's chambers moved in front of the empty jury box.

No jury necessary for Ro's arraignment. The judge would do the work on his own today.

"All rise."

Chatter, that annoying crescendo of mingled voices, stopped. They all stood. Joey leaned in again. "Pray we don't get Jackson. We're cooked if we get him."

To drive the point home, he sliced his hand across his throat and made a slashing noise.

"Sssh."

Lucie glanced over at the Buccarellis on the other side of Dad. Mrs. B. had done her best to put on a full face of makeup and her fancy hair, as she called it, but the pale, puffy skin under her eyes told the story. If Ro didn't get released today, her mother would have to be committed. Unlike the Rizzos, the Buccarellis weren't conditioned for this.

"Court is now in session," the bailiff said in a voice meant to convey he wouldn't take any guff. "The honorable judge Jackson presiding."

Joey let out a grunt and Mom elbowed him.

"Screwed," Dad muttered.

A rotund, gray-haired man with sagging cheeks entered, his robe swaying as he climbed to the bench. "Thank you, everyone. Please be seated."

He situated himself, tucked his glasses on his beak of a nose, and peered around the courtroom, his gaze zooming to Dad. His already slacked cheeks dropped another inch.

Maybe Dad being here wasn't such a good idea.

After a full minute's stare-down, the judge addressed the attorneys. "I'm ready to call the People vs. Buccarelli. The officers will be bringing in Ms. Buccarelli any minute."

The attorneys did their thing, introducing themselves to the judge in the seconds before the side door opened.

Escorted by a guard, Ro stepped into the packed room. She wore orange prison scrubs, her hands and feet shackled. Her long, silky hair had been brushed and the leftover curls she painstakingly styled each morning drooped. Something inside Lucie shattered. Had she ever seen Ro with limp, unwashed hair?

On sleepovers when they were twelve. Maybe. Even on nights when Lucie crashed at Ro's for girl time, Ro always put her hair into a ponytail in the morning.

Their eyes met for a few seconds and Lucie, at a complete loss to find the upshot, gave her a thumbs up. Thumbs up? Really?

A weak smile lifted the corner of Ro's mouth, then she shifted her gaze to mom and finally Joey, where it stayed for a few seconds. Roseanne loved Lucie's idiot brother. Together, they made a good pair. Both nuts, both with flashing tempers, both generous in their own way.

All Lucie needed to do was get Ro out of this mess so that relationship could continue.

Ro faced the judge, giving Lucie the full brunt of the back of her head where she'd missed a few spots with the brush. From the end of the row, Mrs. B. sucked a horrified breath. *Okay, Mrs. B., settle down now. It's just hair.*

The judge requested Ro give her name and address for the court record.

"Ms. Buccarelli, I want to advise you that you're charged on December 7 of this year in Cook County. Count one, homicide, murder in the first degree of Buzzy Sneider. That is a felony punishable by life in prison without parole."

Lucie gasped. Life in prison. Were these people insane?

The judge shot her a look and pointed. "Not another sound, young lady, or I will have you removed." He went back to his notes. "The jury will be permitted to consider lesser included offense of homicide, murder in the second degree. That is a felony punishable by four to twenty years in prison. Do you understand?"

While Lucie fought the urge to scream obscenities, Ro looked at Willie, who nodded. And how sad was it that they'd all learned not to speak unless consulting a lawyer?

"Yes," Ro said.

Maybe Ro understood, but Lucie didn't. At all. Since the judge had already called her out, she just sat shaking her head in mute protest. Could head shaking get her a contempt charge? She'd ask her lawyer, but he was busy at the moment.

The judge flew into a spiel, advising Ro of her rights and asking for her plea.

Not guilty. Of course, not guilty. The whole thing was ridiculous.

"Now," Judge Jackson said, "we'll deal with the issue of bond. Let's hear from the people, Mr. Cole."

The prosecutor cleared his throat, "Thank you, your honor. This is a violent crime. A senseless act that has terrified the community."

Come on! Terrified? *Puh-lease.* Lucie let out a long sigh and the judge smacked his gavel. "Order." He waved the gavel at Lucie. "I warned you already. Don't force me to hold you in contempt."

Whoopsie. Lucie held her hand up in apology and then zipped it across her mouth.

"Thank you, your honor." Mr. Cole said. "Now, I'd like to add that in addition to the fear instilled on the community, we know that Ms. Buccarelli has ties with the Rizzo crime family. We believe Ms. Buccarelli to be a potential flight risk. Given the heinous nature of the crime, we would ask that the court set no bond in this matter."

No bond. That snapped it. The guy must have left his mind on the curb. Ro didn't even have a criminal record and they were painting her to be some violent menace. So unfair. Lucie set her hands on her thighs and squeezed, letting all the tension flow through her fingers.

The judge held a hand to Willie. "Mr. Clay?"

Our turn. Lucie sat a little straighter. Now they'd see the master in action. *Go get 'em, Willie.*

Willie stood and smoothed a hand over his $500 tie. "Thank you, your honor. Ms. Buccarelli is a model citizen who has lived in Cook County her entire life. She has family here and lives within ten miles of the courthouse. She has no prior record. She understands the seriousness of the charges and intends to defend herself passionately. However, it could take months for this case to go to trial. If she is found not guilty of these charges, she could suffer irreparable harm after spending that time in custody. We certainly don't want an innocent woman's life ruined. We request bond be set, even if it is a high bond. Please, your honor, allow Ms. Buccarelli to show this court she intends to return."

The judge eyeballed Ro, then Willie, then the prosecutor. He took a few seconds to review his notes before peeling off his glasses.

"Thank you," he said. "The court has considered these allegations very carefully. They are extremely violent. Also, Ms. Buccarelli's ties with convicted felons must be evaluated."

He made eye contact with Dad and Lucie felt that same burn rise into her chest. Humiliation. Wait. No. *Anger.* This time it wasn't about Dad. It was about Ro and that's all this judge should be considering. Ro shouldn't be punished because she'd been a great friend to a girl whose father made bad—horrible—choices.

"Given the charges and the defendant's lifestyle," the judge continued. "I'm ordering Ms. Buccarelli held without bond."

7

Ro's mom lost it. Just tossed her hands up and threw her body forward, collapsing over the railing dividing her from her daughter.

"My baby," she wailed.

The gallery erupted, reporters chattering, spectators gasping, others applauding. Applauding? What about any of this warranted that?

The full force of noise slammed into Lucie, making her ears ring and her mind race. *No bail, no bail, no bail.*

In the chaos, Ro swung back to her mother. "Mom, it's okay," she said, her voice strong and firm above the courtroom noise. "I'm okay."

"My baby!"

Mr. B. leaped from his seat and poked a beefy finger at the judge. "What a bunch of baloney."

The judge slammed his gavel, banging it hard. "Order. Order in the court."

Good luck with that.

He banged the useless gavel a few more times. "Bailiff! Please remove the defendant."

Excitement over, a crowd of folks made a push for the exit, all of them attempting to squeeze through the double doors at once. Probably all the reporters anxious to get this on tape for the latest breaking news segments.

"My baby," Mrs. B. cried again.

Someone needed to give her a Valium or something. The increased drama would only wind up on the evening news.

The officer who'd escorted Ro into the room grabbed her arm. *Uh-oh.* That wouldn't fly. Lucie whipped her head around and found Joey's face already turning that ugly shade of purple that preceded a meltdown. Crossing herself, she shot off a quick novena.

Couldn't hurt.

"Ho," Joey hollered. "Take it easy with her. She's shackled."

Understanding the nuances of life with Rizzo men, Mom sidestepped and faced her son, her eyes burning. "Don't go crazy in here. I won't have it."

"Joey," Ro shouted. "Lock up my jewelry. And my mink. Don't let that rat bastard stripper-banging ex near the house. Please."

For not the first time, Lucie gawked. *That's* what she was worried about?

The press would get a hundred miles out of this freak show.

The guard kept his grip on Ro, dragging her toward the door as she shuffled along, screaming orders over her shoulder. "Especially the diamond earrings you gave me. Put them in the safe."

After seeing this fiasco on the evening news, thieves everywhere might hunt down Ro's house. And her diamond earrings. One thing Joey wasn't was cheap.

Lucie raised both hands. "Stop talking. We've got it. Don't worry, we'll get you out. I promise."

"I love you, Luce. And Mom and Dad. I love you. Joey. I love you."

"Gotta say," Dad said, "none of my trials got looney like this."

"Dad!"

Her father pulled a *what-did-I-do?* face. "What? It's nuts in here."

Again, the judge slammed his gavel. He might as well cut that out right now. Nothing would tame this bunch.

"*You* oughta get locked up," Mr. B. roared, still jabbing his finger at the judge. "She's a good girl and you put her in with a bunch of lowlifes." He turned to Dad. "No offense, Joe."

"None taken." Dad gently touched Mr. B.'s arm. "But you gotta calm down. I know this judge. He'll throw you in there too."

"Sir," the judge said to Mr. B, "leave this court before I hold you in contempt."

Dad turned to Lucie. "See? Am I right or am I wrong? Loves to cage people, this judge."

Mr. B. gave the judge the stink eye. "Ah, baloney."

"My baby!"

Holy cow. Everyone needed to get a grip. Lucie had already spent time in a cell—twice—and had no interest in going back. If someone got arrested today, it wouldn't be her. Loyalty only took her so far.

The room whirled and Lucie drew a long breath, fought to focus just for a few seconds. They needed a plan.

Everyone out. If she could at least get them all into the fresh air, they could regroup.

"Dad, get Mr. B. out of here. Mom and I will get Mrs. B."

She snapped her fingers at Joey still watching the guard haul Ro away. "Hey, pay attention. We're mission critical here. Help dad. Mom and I will handle Ro's mom."

"My baby!"

Oh, my God. Enough with the "my baby" already.

Joey angled around Mom, set his hand on Mr. B.'s back. "Let's go. As mad as you are, lighting this judge up isn't gonna help. Believe me."

Hang on. Was that Joey, King of the PITAs, talking so rationally? Amazeballs. Maybe there was hope for him yet.

"My baby," Mrs. B. wailed.

Time to move before Ro's mother had a psychotic break. Lucie faced Mom and clutched her forearm. "This is a two-woman job. You're a mother, you talk while I get her up and out the door. We just need to distract her long enough to get her to the door."

Mom nodded. "Honestly, the drama these people create puts the Rizzos to shame. Who'd have believed *that* one?"

IN THE TWENTY MINUTES IT TOOK TO GET MR. AND MRS. B. to their car, Lucie's phone had blown up. Texts, calls, more texts, all of them firing in like machine gun strikes.

Mom glanced at her, eyebrows hiked. "Please shut that off. I can't take anymore."

"Sorry." Not wanting to verbalize that the calls must be about Ro, Lucie jerked her head at Mrs. B. "Everyone must be watching the news or something."

Obliging her mother, she powered the phone down and swung the passenger side door of Mr. B.'s ancient Lincoln open, nudging Mrs. B. into the seat. She strapped her in while the poor woman sobbed. Total wreck.

Seatbelt secure, Lucie stepped back.

"My baby," Mrs. B wailed, once again throwing her body forward and nearly decapitating herself in the process.

Mom propped her hands on her hips. "Maria, knock it off before you hurt yourself. You know we'll get her out of there. Roseanne belongs in jail as much as Lucie does."

Considering Lucie had been arrested a couple months back and incorrectly charged with storing stolen merchandise, Mom's analogy, to say the least, fell flat. Mrs. B. started screaming again.

"How about we not talk?" Lucie shut the car door.

"I was trying to help."

The cold air fell blissfully quiet. Well, as quiet as it could with a deranged woman wailing from the confines of a car. Behind them, Joey and Dad walked up with Mr. B.

"I don't understand," Ro's dad said. "How did this happen?"

"I don't know," Lucie said. "We're having some business issues with Buzzy." Well, not Buzzy anymore. Dead Buzzy. Ew. Whatever. "Uh, Buzzy's company. They swiped a few of Ro's designs and Ro has been...vocal."

"How many times," Dad said, "do I tell my guys to stay off that damned twitting."

Dad. Had to love him.

Joey refrained from correcting Dad, but offered up an eye roll that should have scrambled his brain. "We gotta figure this out."

Dad held his hands up. "Willie is on it. He's got a couple of crack investigators working this 24/7."

"Good," Lucie said. "What about Buzzy's security system? There has to be video."

"It's a bust."

"What does that mean?"

"It must not have been on. Willie found out there's no video from that night."

Damn it. A bit of Lucie's hope took a blast on that one. But they'd press forward. Figure something else out. "I'll look into a few things," she said. "All it'll take is something, anything, to clear her of suspicion. She met with the buyer at Frampton's around the same time that Buzzy died. I'll call the client, verify she was with them and we're done." Lucie smacked her hands together. "Over. Ro is free."

Because one thing was for sure. Lucie couldn't sit around while Ro became someone's prison bitch.

ON A MISSION TO SCOUR RO'S COMPUTER AND CALENDAR, Lucie left the courthouse and headed straight for the office. She'd spent hours last night combing through her BFF's various email folders only to realize she'd taken for granted how much Ro accomplished in a day. When this was over, a raise was in order. Whatever cushion existed in Lucie's budget would be Ro's increase.

Done.

The drive to the office kept her from responding to the flurry of texts and phone calls streaming in, but she'd get to them when she stopped moving.

She pushed through the office door and Lauren, one of her part-timers, hopped up from behind Ro's desk.

"Oh, my God," she said in that typical fast-moving college girl way. "Did you get my message?"

"No. I've had fifty calls in the last hour."

Lucie marched to Ro's desk bent on a full audit of the computer.

Except...no computer.

Before her butt hit the chair, she pointed to the empty space where Ro's laptop usually sat. "Where's the laptop?"

"*That's* what I was calling about. The police came here. They had a warrant. They took it. And a bunch of other stuff too. I called and called. I didn't know what to do."

A warrant. *Damn it*. Poor Lauren. Here all by herself as cops paraded through. Lucie, never one to get touchy-feely with her employees, set her hand on the girl's shoulder. "Thank you, but there was nothing either of us could have done."

Because Joe Rizzo's daughter knew a thing or thirty about warrants. "If they had a warrant, we wouldn't have been able to stop them."

"I know, but it seems so wrong that they can just take anything they want. They even took her sketch pad."

Ugh. The sketch pad. Ro loved that thing. A fan of spiral notebooks, she'd opted for an oversized spiral pad that she could flip back and forth on. She'd ordered them in bulk because she said it was good karma. That all those sketch pads meant a lot of ideas.

Lucie may have owned Coco Barknell, but Ro's designs and salesmanship had gotten them their biggest client. In business and in friendship, they were partners.

The doggie bells jangled and Tim entered the shop. Given that it was barely 3:00, he still wore the same suit from that morning. The gray one with the light blue tie that brought out the red in his hair. She loved that suit on him. Really, she loved anything on Tim.

He strode toward her, his broad shoulders pushed back in that familiar way that made Lucie believe he could carry just about anything on them.

Even her drama.

The overhead light caught the glint of his badge and sidearm at his waist. The whole look, the confidence, the presence, brought an odd mix of security and lust.

Tim. Tim. Tim.

"Hi," she said. "Did you hear about Ro?"

He set his big hands on her shoulders and kissed her. Nothing too crazy in front of Lauren, but a soft brush of his lips that made Lucie yearn to curl into him.

He backed away from the kiss and nodded. "I'm sorry."

Weren't they all.

She didn't want apologies though. She wanted to understand. "How is that possible when she doesn't have a criminal record?"

Tim stayed quiet. Of course he did. They'd been through this same routine plenty of times. One of the many things she loved, simply adored, about him was his honesty. His loyalty to the job. Tim didn't allow himself to be manipulated or used, and he never compromised his ethics by sharing information about his cases.

Ever.

For months now, she'd been respecting those boundaries and making sure her father and brother did the same. Tim would not be one of their insiders in the PD. No way.

Except now, with Ro behind bars, she sort of wanted him to pony up. Leave it to her to fall in love with an honorable guy.

Totally aggravating.

"It's up to the judge," he finally said.

Which she knew. "That judge hates us."

"He doesn't hate you."

Oh, please. "You weren't there. You didn't see how he

looked at my dad. That's what this is about. He's punishing Ro because of Dad, well, that won't fly. No sir."

"What does that mean?"

"Nothing."

"Luce, stay out of it."

"I'm not doing anything."

Tim laughed. "Nice try. I know you." He grabbed her hands and squeezed. "Please, I'm begging you, stay out of it. Homicide is on it. If she's innocent..."

What *if*? Did Tim think? Oh, come on. "If? Are you kidding me?"

He held his hands flat in front of him. That *holy-crap-settle-down* gesture alpha men liked to employ.

"*When,*" he said. "When she's proven innocent, she'll be released. For now, don't go off on one of your screwball investigations."

Good luck there, pal. Still...she met his gaze, grabbed onto his hands and squeezed. "Kinda hard to do a screwball investigation when fifty percent of the screwball is behind bars."

VISITOR'S PASS SECURED, LUCIE PRESSED THREE ON THE elevator leading up to the Foo-Foo Entertainment corporate floor and stepped back while Joey corralled their most recent dog walking client, a fifty-five pound, tan terrier/labradoodle mix named Coitus. This poor dog wound up with a pothead owner who thought it funny that the animal humped everything he set his sights on. Thus, Rodney became Coitus. Idiot pothead changed the dog's name at two years old.

Poor guy. The dog. Not the pothead.

Oy. 9:00 a.m. might be too early for Lucie to deal with a humping dog named Coitus.

But they needed props for this impromptu meeting at Foo-Foo Entertainment and Coitus lived around the block.

The elevator doors slid closed. Lucie stood back, eyeballing her charges: Boots, an adorable Bijon Frise-Yorkie mix with ears that stuck straight out like airplane wings when he got excited, and Brie, a spoiled Griffon Bruxellois owned by a famous chef who'd just hired Coco Barknell for dog walking services.

Joey leaned against the wall while Coitus sized up Brie.

"Control him," she said. "He's salivating over Brie."

"He's fine. Tell me again what we're doing here?"

"If we want to get Ro out, we need evidence to support her case. The victim's workplace is a good jumping off point. Besides, Buzzy has—had—five billion assistants. We'll start with Reece and see where that takes us. She might give up some gossip on Buzzy. Someone was mad enough to kill her, and Reece was the most senior assistant. If anyone knows anything, it'll be her. Besides, we still need models for the fashion show. We're doing double duty here."

"This fashion show is a pain in the ass."

"You're telling me. I didn't appreciate how much Ro did for me before this. Anyway, just roll with it. Reece thinks we're here to show her models."

Coitus took two steps toward Brie. Lucie pointed at him. "Sit, Coitus."

When he didn't move, Joey rolled his eyes. "Sit, Coitus. You horny bastard."

Coitus planted his butt. Why did it always work when Joey said it? Totally irritating.

The elevator door whooshed open, and Lucie led the charge down the long corridor to Buzzy's office. Six of her assistants worked in the bullpen just outside it. Shouting distance, Buzzy had once joked.

Reece stepped into the hallway. She wore a navy dress and tights with a pair of fun clunky boots. Edgy, yet professional. A look Lucie always admired, but could never pull off.

Reece waved. "Good morning."

"Hi, Reece." Without a free hand, Lucie jerked her head to Joey. "I don't think you've met my brother, Joey. And this is, Brie and Boots and, um…"

Lord, she didn't even want to say it.

"Coitus," Joey added. "The name sucks, but you get used to it."

Reece burst out laughing. "*Coitus? That's…*unbelievable."

And that's when Coitus sniffed the air, mounted Reece's calf, and went to work.

"Coitus," Lucie said. "No. Off!"

Joey grabbed hold of the dog, gently pulling him from Reece's leg. "I'm sorry."

"I've nicknamed him Super Perv," Lucie said. "But he's cute. He'd be a great fit for the skiwear segment of the show."

Unperturbed, Reece gave Coitus a tickle under his chin. "You're a naughty boy, Coitus."

She stood tall and motioned them to the board room in the corner. "Let's take them to the conference room. One of the staff members wants us to look at her poodle also. Buzzy used her in some of the Foo-Foo ads, so she'd probably be a good addition."

Poodle. Lucie thought back to samples of Foo-Foo commercials she'd compiled while deciding on whether or not to partner with Buzzy. "Is that the one with the pink bows in her hair?"

"Yes. That's her."

"Oh, she's a cutie."

Kandi, another of Buzzy's assistants who'd been helping with the fashion show, stepped out of an office carrying a box that tipped precariously.

"Hey, Lucie. How are you?"

"I'm good, Kandi. That looks heavy."

She boosted the box only to have it wobble. Joey shoved Coitus' leash at Lucie and grabbed the box. Aw, such a gentleman. This was the Joey she loved.

In a burst of action, Coitus lunged forward, tugging so hard he knocked Lucie—the lightweight—off balance. *Ooooff!* What the heck?

Momentum carried her, her body tipping forward. Rather than faceplant on top of Boots and Brie and get dragged, she let go of the leash, catching herself on the doorframe before she crushed the dogs.

Coitus shot off to the end of the hallway, his fifty-five pounds in a full charge. And then Lucie saw why.

At the end of the hallway stood the adorable poodle, her curly hair all pinned up in pink bows. She wore a pink sweater with a fur collar that easily could have been one of Ro's designs. All this dog needed was some pink lipstick.

Coitus. *Ohmygod.*

"No, Coitus. Coitus!"

Joey spun back, set the box on the closest desk, and hauled butt just as Lucie shoved the leashes at Kandi.

But...too late. Coitus got there first and, at twice the size of the poodle, leaped, tackling the poor baby and, yep... hump, hump, humped away as the poodle barked and made a weird noise.

Wait. Was that...moaning? *Ew.*

Doggie porn just got added to the audio porn library.

The poodle's owner, a middle-aged woman with dark hair pulled into a severe bun stepped in, shoving Coitus away with one hand and scooping the poodle up with the other. "Pig!"

She cuddled the poodle against her, murmuring something Lucie couldn't hear.

Lucie skidded to a stop, only to be plowed into by her mountain of a brother. She tumbled forward. The woman hopped clear as Lucie slammed into one of the padded cubicle walls, bounced off, and landed flat on her rear on the floor. "Ow."

Her sit bones took the brunt of it and pain ricocheted down her legs. *Damned, Coitus.* Boots and Brie jumped on top of her, leaping up and licking her chin, and the dual doggie bath made the pain in Lucie's rear disappear.

The violated poodle's owner poked her finger. "That dog is disgusting."

"I'm so sorry." Lucie set Boots and Brie on the floor, held the leashes in one hand and levered up. "Bad, Coitus!"

Coitus had apparently not reached the promised land. If he couldn't have the poodle, the owner would have to do. He wrapped his front paws around the woman's pant leg and shot off a rapid humping while Lucie stood paralyzed in horror.

"Off," Joey said, using his alpha voice.

The dog hopped off—literally—and stood at attention, his gaze on Joey, who bent low and grabbed the leash.

The woman held onto her beloved poodle, stroking her head and murmuring. The poodle though, didn't seem all that freaked. No shivering, no look of rampant terror. In fact, if Lucie were to guess, she'd think that poodle didn't mind the action.

"I am so sorry," Lucie said to the woman.

"That dog needs to be fixed."

"He is fixed," Joey added. "He's just horny."

Reece hustled up behind Lucie. "This is nuts. Let's get the dogs into the conference room before one of the VPs comes out screaming."

Once confined to the conference room, a large space that fit at least twenty, they let the dogs roam free. Reece shook her head and laughed. "Wow. That was a scene. I think the poodle liked it. With an owner like Flora, who could blame her? She never lets that dog have any fun."

Lucie snorted. "I really am sorry."

"It's all right. Crazier things have happened here."

Really? What exactly did that mean? "Well, that's good to know, but I can't imagine it would be worse than that."

"Please. You should have been here the day—" Reece caught herself.

Damn it. "The day what?"

She glanced up at the corner of the room, and Lucie tracked her gaze to a video camera mounted high on the wall.

"Um, nothing," Reece said. "Nothing."

Clearly, she didn't want to speak in front of the camera. Was someone listening as well as watching?

"Anyway," Reece said, "we're thinking these three dogs for the fashion show? And the poodle, yes?"

"I think Boots, Brie, and the poodle. Coitus will have to sit this one out. He can't be trusted."

At the end of the table, Joey squatted and gave Coitus a pat on the back. "So harsh. These women don't understand, buddy."

"Hush up down there. Don't even start."

At that, Reece smiled. "You two are funny."

That was one word for it. "You should see him and Ro together. They're dating."

"Really? I didn't know that." She met Joey's gaze. "I'm so sorry. About Ro."

Joey shrugged. "She didn't do it. We'll get her out."

Speaking of which… "Reece, I don't want to put you in a tough spot, but there's no way Ro could have done this. You spent a ton of time with Buzzy, can you think of anything that might clear Ro? Please, we can't let an innocent woman go to prison."

The room fell silent, all the thick, stifling tension drowning out any sound. Reece's gaze went to the camera then flicked back to Lucie. She checked her watch.

"You know, I just remembered another meeting. We'll have to cut this short. I'll walk you out."

What? After that impassioned plea, she wouldn't give up any info?

Come on!

Joey collected the dogs and handed Boots and Brie off to Lucie while Reece manned the door. As Lucie approached, Reece met her stare, their eyes holding for a long second. What the message in those eyes was, Lucie couldn't tell.

"We know the way out," Lucie said.

"No. I'll walk you down."

Huh. Now this was interesting.

On the elevator, Reece hit L, waited for the doors to close and turned to Lucie. "I couldn't talk in the conference room. I think they record our conversations."

"Is that even legal?"

Reece shrugged. "No idea." She shifted to Joey. "I really am sorry about Ro. I like her. I'll try to help, but I can't talk here. I won't risk them overhearing. Who knows what they do with all those recordings."

Yes! Maybe this visit hadn't been a complete bust. "Rizzos," Lucie said. "Can you meet us there?"

Lauren checked her watch. "I have a meeting at ten. How about 11:30?"

8

———

Lucie and Joey walked into the downtown location of Rizzo's Italian Beef at 11:10. She'd wanted to show up early to beat the lunch crowd and grab a table along the wall. Away from the activity.

Wasn't every day she talked murder with someone.

At this point, Lucie should start a memoir on the stream of oddball occurrences in her life. A girl couldn't make this nonsense up.

Joey detoured to the kitchen to visit with the employees and, well, create his normal brand of upheaval. Lucie plopped down at a corner table to check messages. Without Ro to manage the office, she'd put Mom on duty while Lauren covered the day's pooch walks. Not for the first time, Lucie missed the early days when she was the sole employee of Coco Barknell. Back then it had simply been Lucie's Dog Walking. It all started with Otis. Then, with Ro's help, they'd expanded Lucie's hobby of making fancy jewel studded collars to a bonafide business. One that now provided an entire line of doggie coats and collars to a major department store. Not to mention the online retail sales and the handful of boutiques that sold their wares.

All because Ro had the gumption and style to aid Lucie's launch of Coco Barknell.

And now she sat in a cell. *I have to get her out.*

"Hi, Lucie."

Lucie glanced up and found Reece standing beside her. She wore a black knee-length coat and a red scarf with giant creepy clown faces all over it. Alrighty, then.

Before sitting, Reece scanned the restaurant as if expecting an ambush of some sort.

Lucie held one hand out. "Joey is in the kitchen talking to some friends. Would you like something to eat?"

"No. I'm good thanks. I need to get back to the office soon."

Reece unbuttoned her coat but didn't remove it. Obviously in a hurry.

"Sorry to bug you, but thanks for coming out."

"No problem. I feel horrible for Roseanne."

"Me too. There's no way she did this. I've known her my entire life—she doesn't have it in her."

"I believe you. I'm just not sure what I can tell you. Buzzy made me sign a non-disclosure agreement."

Now that was interesting. "I see. Well, I don't want to get you in legal trouble. How about I just ask some questions and you tell me if you can't answer?"

"Sure. That works."

Being a type A personality, Lucie had prepared a list and memorized it. "As you're aware, there are some issues concerning Foo-Foo selling our designs. I'm curious if there are other products where something similar has happened."

"Sorry. I can't comment on that."

Okay. This might be a bigger challenge than expected. She'd have to figure it out though. Get at least a small lead on who might be mad enough at Buzzy to kill her. How to get there though?

Reece tapped her fingers on the table. "I can comment on things that have been reported on in the news media. That's already out there."

Aha. Lucie held a finger in triumph. "Excellent. Let's go with that. Buzzy was a public person. I'm sure she had plenty of nutjobs contacting her. Has there been anything in the news lately that she'd been concerned about?"

Reece twisted her lips one way, then the other. *Uh-oh.* Lucie must not have asked the right question. "What about the people who work for her? Any reports or rumors about that?"

"Um, if you check the entertainment news outlets, you might find a rumor that she wanted to fire her agent."

Lucie snatched her phone from her purse and searched for Buzzy's agent's name. A full page of links popped up. Ooooh-wee, there'd apparently been some scuttlebutt about the agent's business practices.

Reece sat forward, peeked over both shoulders, and Lucie contained an eye roll. This wasn't a top-secret briefing for heaven's sake.

"It wasn't Buzzy," Reece said.

"I'm sorry?"

"Buzzy liked her agent. It was Lorraine who didn't like him."

Given Lorraine's protective tendencies, that made sense. In the initial meeting with Buzzy, Lorraine had sat in, peppering Lucie and Ro with questions. Considering the lot Lucie came from, nothing about it struck her as odd. The questions were low-key, politically correct versions of Joey's *touch-my-sister-and-I'll-kick-your-ass*.

Still, if Lorraine had issues with the agent, Lucie assumed there were reasons. "Why didn't she like him?"

"As you'll see when you do the research, she thought he was stealing from Buzzy."

Stealing. *Well, well, well.* "I see."

Reece nodded. "Things like taking a bigger cut of deals than he was supposed to or floating some of her money as a —" she made air quotes, "—loan."

Money. Always the problem.

Ideas popped into Lucie's mind. All the ways a relationship could shatter when money was involved. "Did they fire him?"

"No. Buzzy loved him."

"She trusted him even after he stole from her?"

Reece waggled her hand. "Gray area. There was no real proof he stole. For the deals he made, the money came through his agency. He'd take his percentage and send Buzzy the balance."

"So how was he stealing? I'm sure the paper trail showed how much she should have made."

"It did. The issue was in the...timing...of when he sent the money. That's really all I can say."

Given her finance background, Lucie understood. "He held on to the money, earned interest on it, and then cut her a check."

If true, that could have been a lot of money. Buzzy's net worth had been a reported $550 million.

"Hello, ladies."

Oh, boy.

At the sound of her father's voice, Lucie glanced up. When did he ever step into the restaurant he owned?

The entire city knew the place was a front—one that failed to keep him out of prison—so he could show legitimate income.

He stood next to the table in black slacks with a crease so sharp it could have beheaded someone and a white dress shirt with the top two buttons undone. Since getting out of prison, he'd gained ten pounds. The weight had filled out his angular face, and he'd let his hair grow a tad longer so he could comb it straight back and have it stay in place. The old Joe. The dapper, media darling Joe. Notoriety, charm, and the olive-skinned good looks that made movie stars legends.

He was a legend all right.

Across from her, Reece's eyes got big. Lucie couldn't blame her. How often did one come face to face with the most notorious Chicago mob boss since Al Capone?

"Dad, this is Reece."

"Nice to meet you. I got some food on the way."

"Um," Reece said, "I need to get back to work. Thank you though."

"Eh. You'll take it to go then."

Reece stood, her fingers automatically going to her coat buttons. She made quick work of the job and rewrapped the creepy clown scarf around her neck.

Joey approached the table carrying two trays loaded with sandwiches and fries. Before the tray even hit the table, Lucie inhaled the aroma of roasted beef and herbs. Add the fresh fried potatoes and...maybe she could eat. Honestly, who did her father think would consume all this? Joey ate like a dinosaur, but he and Tim combined couldn't handle that much food.

They loaded Reece up with bags of food and she scooted before Lucie could ask any follow-up questions. *Thanks, Dad.*

Never one to let an opportunity pass, Dad commandeered Reece's seat. Joey plunked down next to him.

"You two eat." Dad looked at Lucie. "Especially you. Put a little meat on those bones."

"Dad!"

"What? It wouldn't hurt you to eat a little more. At least now you don't look like we starve you. Moving back home put weight on you."

Beside her, Joey snorted and Dad gave him a winning smile.

"Hey, Joe," a man called as he strode by with his tray of food.

"Oh, hey," Dad said. "Good to see you. Thanks for coming in."

Dad's fan club. All it took was one person to kick off a chorus of hellos.

And it begins...

Lucie unwrapped a sandwich—no sense letting it go to waste—and popped a fry into her mouth. "Dad, what are you doing here?"

"I followed you."

Mid-chew, Lucie gulped her food down. "You *followed* us?"

"Yeah. When your mother said she was working at your office, I wanted to know what you were doing."

Seriously, she needed to move out of Villa Rizzo. "I'm trying to get Ro out of jail."

"Tim know about this?"

"I'm not talking about Tim."

"He doesn't know. Better that way."

Only a mob boss would think keeping secrets about a murder investigation was a good thing.

"The broad that just left, who is she?" Dad's mouth dipped. "She needs a nicer scarf. I mean, clowns?"

Again Joey let out a laugh. These two.

Lucie munched another fry. "She works for Buzzy Sneider's company. She said there was drama between Buzzy's sister and agent. I'll call Buzzy's sister and see if I can set up a meeting. I'll tell her in light of the tragedy, I'd like to see if we can resolve this issue about the designs Buzzy stole. God rest her soul."

"Good. I'll go with you."

"Oh, I don't think so."

Dad smacked his fingers against the edge of the table. "You think I'd let you talk to this woman alone? With her sister in a morgue?" He shook his head. "No. I'm going."

Beside her, Joey took a massive bite of his sandwich, his gaze shooting between Dad and Lucie. Help from him wouldn't come. That'd be the day Joey went against Dad.

"We'll talk about it later," Lucie said.

"Eh. You talk, I won't listen. We'll go see the sister. Case closed."

Lorraine Sneider was holding court in her brownstone. The one neighboring her sister's.

God, that would be awful. Coming home every night, passing your sibling's home knowing she'd been murdered inside. Lucie wouldn't have been able to do it. She'd have to move. Some things were simply outside the natural order of life.

After ditching Joey at Rizzo's, Lucie and Dad drove up to Buzzy and Lorraine's street in cushy Lincoln Park and found both ends of the block barricaded by uniformed officers. Reporters and cameramen blanketed the area, vying for the best possible spot near the front of the pack.

"Vultures," Dad said. "Baby girl, you have no idea."

Her father. The superstar.

"Nor do I want to, Dad."

Dad nudged into a no-parking zone on the corner and was rewarded with a shot of the bird from an annoyed cameraman who'd been pushed from a prime viewing space.

Calmly, Dad hit the window button and stuck his head out. "Do it again and I'll break that finger off."

Oy. Time to go. Lucie had learned keeping Dad focused avoided distractions like punching the lights out of random strangers who might press charges.

If she worked quickly enough, she'd eliminate any further interaction between the bird-flipper and her fiery father.

She yanked the door handle. "I'll talk to the cop and see if we can get through."

"Awright. I'll wait here with the car. Drop my name. If I know this cop, it might help."

Ohmygod.

A lawsuit, Ro locked up, and Lucie running shotgun with Dad. How did this become her life?

Lucie hopped out of the car, pushed through a couple of reporters, and marched right up to the beat cop. "Hi."

The cop, a middle-aged guy with jowly cheeks gave her thick-soled boots, jeans, and down jacket the once-over.

"If you're a protester, I don't want to hear it."

A protester? She glanced down at her ensemble, decided nothing about it said protestor, and faced the cop again.

"No. I'm actually a business partner of Buzzy's." She dug

a business card and driver's license from her purse and handed it over. "Lucie *Rizzo* from Coco Barknell. I wanted to pay my respects to Lorraine."

Such a name dropper.

The cop studied the card. "Rizzo? Are you—"

"Lucie Rizzo. Yes." She did jazz hands. "That's me."

The cop laughed. "Listen, toots, a little tip, if you want to get through here, don't be a ballbuster."

He was right. Wasn't his fault she'd endured a lifetime of people looking down on her because of her father's legal woes.

"Hey," someone behind her yelled. "Where are *you* going?"

That brought a chorus of shouts and—oh, no. She couldn't look. Couldn't.

"Is there a man walking toward us. Salt and pepper hair, nice overcoat? Kind of distinguished looking?"

Being the peanut she was, the cop peered across the top of her head. "Whoa," he said. "Is that..."

Damn it, Dad.

Lucie whipped back. Her father exchanged words with one of the reporters, whose eyes suddenly grew wide, his head bobbing up and down. One thing about her father, he knew how to make an entrance.

"Dad!"

Her father flashed her a wide smile, held his finger up, said one last thing to the reporter, then made his way toward her and the cop.

"Sorry," he said, "I had to straighten something out."

He reached his hand to the cop. "Joe Rizzo. Good to meet you."

Her father. The master. With very little effort, by simply holding his hand out and introducing himself, he'd just shoved this cop into a corner. If the cop ignored the gesture, he'd appear rude. And what person in their right mind would be rude to a mob boss? Particularly if said mob boss had been perfectly polite.

Please, please, please shake his hand.

Because her father's charm had a short leash. In a few seconds, the famous Joe Rizzo might fly into a vein-popping rage over this cop refusing to shake his hand. For all his faults, and God knew there were plenty, common courtesy was a hot button with her father. If he treated you well, he expected the same in return.

Even if he was crazy.

The cop finally shook his hand and Lucie let out a quiet rush of air.

Wasn't this the dilemma she'd fought for so long? The two sides of her father. On the one side she saw a man who'd provided for his family, gave them every material thing they'd ever needed. On the other side? The man who'd lied—by omission—to his children about how he made his living and had committed crimes Lucie didn't want to think about.

She couldn't be naive about it, though. Men didn't climb the ranks of the mob with their charity work.

Even if he did collect toys for needy kids at Christmas.

Dad let go of the cop's hand and turned to Lucie. "What's the hold up? I'm in a no-parking zone. And if I don't move, this nice officer is going to give me a ticket."

Nice officer?

This was a switch.

He went back to the cop. "Look, my daughter wants to visit the dead broad's sister, but this place is nuts right now. There's no parking anywhere and I'm not leaving her here with these vultures. Can we let her through and, when I know she's safe, I'll go move my car?"

Go Dad.

The cop eyed Dad, then shifted to Lucie, who did her best with a demure, pleading smile. *Academy Awards, here we come.*

"Hold on," one of the reporters said. "I think that's Joe Rizzo."

"Joe," a man yelled.

"Joe, what are you doing here?"

"Joe, did you know, Buzzy?"

Joe, Joe, Joe.

A weird pressure built in the air, one Lucie hadn't felt since the day of her father's sentencing. Reporters had circled around them, shoving closer and closer, ripping the oxygen away, while jabbing microphones in their faces, seeking that all important sound bite. Lucie glanced behind her. The mass of people squeezed in, reporters and cameramen once again vying for position. A few more steps and they'd be ensnared.

Get out. Walk away.

The feeling from that day in court, the tightness in her chest, the racing mind, the panic, it all came back to her.

"Crap." The cop shoved by Lucie and Dad. "Quiet down!"

The shouts died down to a murmur. Well, how about that? This guy was *good.*

"All of you," the cop hollered, "step back. Two steps. Right now."

He waited a few seconds and when nobody moved he shook his head. "Back row. Move it before I start throwing you out for blocking traffic."

That's all it took. The crowd stirred, all of them unhappy kindergartners backing away in unison.

The cop brought his attention to Lucie and her father again. "Hang tight."

His eye still on the crowd, he stepped away, speaking into the radio strapped to his shoulder. He held her business card in front of him, presumably reading her name off. After pausing for a good two minutes, his fingers tapping against her card, he returned.

"Okay," he said. "You can go in. Just you. Walk around the barricade though. There's another officer at the door. He'll check you in."

Check her in? Did she get a name badge too?

Lucie and Dad headed to the edge of the barricade, the cop eyeing them to make sure only Lucie went in.

"Baby girl, you'll have to go alone."

Pity that. Still, her father had helped her. "I know. I'll be fine, Dad. Thank you."

"You're welcome. I'll go back to the car. Circle for a while. You be careful."

"I will."

She ducked around the barricade as another wave of *Joe, Joe, Joe's* started. If nothing else, her father knew how to divert attention.

Having met with Buzzy in her home office three weeks ago, Lucie headed for the middle of the block to Buzzy's brownstone. Its stone facade and intricately carved details made it an absolute showstopper. She'd even added an iron fence anchored with stone pillars around her dormant patch of lawn. Everything about this block, including the sidewalks, screamed clean and bright. And money. Lots of it.

Crime scene tape still hung across the front gate. A shiver ran down Lucie's neck. Buzzy had been murdered here. Right here.

Lucie kept moving, her gaze on the officer near the front

gate of Lorraine's almost identical house. When she reached him, she handed over her ID.

He studied it—as if someone had mugged her and stolen her ID on a barricaded street crawling with cops?—, then stepped aside and waved her in.

9

———

A young woman opened the front door. Something ticked in Lucie's brain. A staffer. Lucie had seen her at the corporate office when they'd initially met with Buzzy.

"Hello," the woman said. "Come in. Lorraine is in the study. I think. I'll take your coat."

The setup of the home was similar to Buzzy's. Staircase to the right. Living room to the left connected to a small study in the middle. Kitchen and dining room at the back end of the house. Lucie glanced into the living room where a crush of people, all dressed in designer suits and dresses formed small groups and murmured softly to each other.

Without waiting for her to surrender, the woman peeled Lucie's jacket off her shoulders. "Um, thanks. Wow, there's a lot of people here."

"This is the early crowd. Wait until tonight. The place will be standing room only. There's food in the kitchen if you want something."

There went the intended private meeting with Lorraine.

A wildly underdressed Lucie dove into the crowd, cutting through the living room toward the study. A giant oak sliding door had been pushed open and tucked behind an arched wall. In the corner, Buzzy's parrot, Felix, a cute Kelly green guy with a splash of yellow feathers on his head, perched inside his cage, his head swaying back and forth.

Lucie and Ro had met him on their first visit to Buzzy's, and Ro had fallen madly in love. For kicks, Buzzy liked teaching the little guy swear words and when he got rolling, he'd make a military unit blush.

Fascinated, she paused for a second, watching him dip and roll his head in perfect time with the soft music streaming from hidden speakers. Was he...*dancing*?

Felix went still and cocked his head, his beady black eyes zooming to hers.

"Hi," she said.

"Don't fucking do it! 5511! Piss off!"

The murmurs in the room ceased and a horrified Lucie glanced left where a man and woman gave her the stink eye.

"Don't fucking do it," the parrot squawked again. "5511! Piss off!

"Holy cow," Lucie said. "What a potty mouth."

"Don't fucking do it!"

Compelled to defend herself, Lucie held her hands out for all the guests to see. "I'm not doing anything. I promise."

"Don't fucking do it!"

Wow. This is what Joey would call a crazy-assed bird. Maybe she'd just walk away. Still holding her hands out, she sidestepped. "Sorry to disturb, little guy. Go back to your dancing."

"That bird," Lorraine said, rushing from the crowd. "He's crazy."

Lorraine wore a black dress with a chunky gold necklace and matching earrings.

She slipped a cover over the cage. "Hi, Lucie. I'm so sorry

about Felix. I think he's stressed with all the people in the house."

"It's no problem. I feel bad for him. He must miss her. If birds are anything like dogs, he might be adjusting to being moved from next door."

"Don't fucking do it!"

Conversation from the crowd, bless their hearts, rose above Felix's tirade. Lorraine latched onto Lucie's elbow, drawing her away. She found a free bit of space next to an oversized floor lamp in the back corner of the room and faced Lucie. Up close like this, the dark shadows under her eyes reminded Lucie to tread carefully. The woman had just lost her only sibling.

"Thank you for coming, Lucie. I know Buzzy was excited to be working with you on the fashion show."

Yeah, and stealing Ro's designs.

"But, honestly, with the developments, are you sure you should be here? Business is one thing, but this is personal."

"Developments?"

"The arrest?"

"Lorraine, I've known Roseanne since grade school. She couldn't have done this. She wouldn't."

Plus, her BFF didn't resort to wedgies. If Ro wanted to kill someone, she wouldn't waste her energy on a wedgie. She'd just shoot 'em and be done with it.

Not that Ro would do that.

Lorraine blinked. "Well, Roseanne has been *upset*."

"And rightly so, wouldn't you say?"

"*If* those allegations are true, of course, but we've yet to determine that. I don't know that this is the time, but I'd like to settle that bit of nasty business. I don't want it tarnishing my sister's memory."

Lucie glanced around at the milling guests. All these

folks here to pay their respects. For whatever reason, she wondered just how many of them were business contacts, like her. Why did it matter? The woman was dead. Murdered right next door.

"I'd like to settle it as well. Should I call Darren and see if we can all set up a meeting?"

Throwing Buzzy's agent's name out there couldn't hurt. At the very least, it would indicate his level of involvement.

Lorraine broke eye contact and scanned the room, waving to one of the guests and offering a tight, controlled smile. "Darren won't be handling any of my sister's affairs from now on. We've decided to go a different way."

Huh. No Darren. Maybe that intel on Buzzy's agent being on the outs wasn't a rumor.

"All right," Lucie said. "Once things die—" She winced at her own poor word choice. "Once things settle down, I'll give you a call and we'll see what we can work out. Foo-Foo Entertainment is still a sponsor, along with Coco Barknell, and I want to make sure it all goes well."

The tension in Lorraine's cheeks eased and she gently squeezed Lucie's arm. "Thank you, Lucie. I adored my sister and I don't want a misunderstanding destroying her legacy. I'm glad you came by today. You surprised me, but I'm pleased we could talk."

Lorraine wandered off to her next guest, leaving Lucie in the corner by herself.

"Don't fucking do it!"

That crazy bird. Even with the cage cover on he wanted to be heard. God help the person who inherited that thing.

Wanting to avoid going near the cage, Lucie ducked out the side door into the hallway. By now Dad would be checking his watch, and she wanted to get outside before he incited a riot. Maybe Dad should take the bird. The two of them together would drive the world insane.

Still, this solo mission had netted a possible resolution to their stolen designs problem and, more importantly, confirmation that Buzzy's agent was on the outs.

All she needed to know was if his banishment would drive him to murder.

DAD PULLED UP IN FRONT OF COCO BARKNELL AND DOUBLE parked behind a Franklin police cruiser, also double parked behind Jimmy Two-Toes' new Cadillac. It was a wonder traffic even flowed.

Not waiting for Dad to shut the engine, Lucie hopped out and scooted into the office. Mom was chatting with Joey, who'd planted his butt at Ro's desk. Lucie had called him, asking that he swing by so they could huddle up. With Ro in jail, Lucie needed help and Joey was, much to her own horror, the defacto Ro.

"Hi," she said.

"Hi, honey," Mom said. "Where's your father?"

"He said he needed to talk to one of the guys down at Petey's."

Secretly, she was glad. Did that make her horrible? She'd just spent the last few, surprisingly not miserable, hours with Dad. Now she needed space. And calm. A Zen moment.

With Joey in residence, that Zen moment might be a stretch. "How's everything here? Anything I need to know?"

"Coitus," Joey said, "he's a pain in the ass."

"Joseph. Language." Mom handed over a stack of messages.

Lucie perused the first one. A potential dog walking client. "You say that about all the dogs."

"This time I mean it. You saw it yourself this morning. And listen, the schedule is getting tight."

"I know."

"Then do something about it."

The dog walking side of the business continued to grow, right along with the accessory side. To date, Lucie delegated most of the walking duties and scheduling to Joey, who didn't want to admit he enjoyed the work. She knew. You didn't live under the same roof with someone for most of your life and not know when they were having fun. She'd hired two part-timers to help as well, but their schedules often collided.

"Is it time to suck it up and hire a full-timer?"

Joey propped his feet on Ro's desk. "It's been time for three months. We're maxed out and Lauren is taking extra credits next semester. If anything, her hours will go down."

"I'd hate to lose her, though. She's good with the dogs."

Joey held his hands out. "You're the one wanting to run a Fortune 500 company."

Lucie dropped the messages on her desk. "How about you, Mom? Anything I need to know?"

"Nope. Just another day in paradise. I worked on a few of the samples Ro requested." Mom pointed to the conference table. "They're over there. Once you sign off, I'll start working on production."

Production. Listen to Mom.

Joey stood and leaned against one of the support beams. "Dad called and said you talked to Buzzy's sister? What the hell?"

She spent two minutes bringing them up to speed then paused to gather her thoughts. "I think we need to look into the agent. Based on the money Buzzy made, he can't be happy about being shoved out."

Roseanne had already spent two days—46 hours to be exact—in jail. And weren't the first 48 hours of an investigation the most critical? She'd heard that on television and it seemed to make sense. As time went on and Ro spent more time behind bars, the possibility existed that the police would stop looking for the real killer. Maybe they had already.

The doggie bells jangled and Lucie glanced up, expecting to see Dad. Instead, her hunky red-headed detective strode in. His suit jacket hung open, his tie was missing—probably hanging from the rearview mirror in his car—and he'd unbuttoned the top two buttons of his shirt. Her fingers immediately itched to touch him.

O'Hottie wore the look well. Really well. "Hey, handsome," she said. "This is a nice surprise."

Tim stopped in front of her and dropped a peck on her lips. No sense making a spectacle in front of Joey and Mom.

"I took a couple of hours personal time. Thought we'd grab a movie and dinner to get your mind off...things."

The robbery case he'd been working had eaten up a lot of his schedule over the past few days. And with Ro's arrest, she'd missed him. But this was life with a man in law enforcement. When the phone rang, he went. No matter what. Something she was still adjusting to.

"Dinner?"

She glanced at Joey. They hadn't finished their strategy session about Buzzy's agent.

Joey waved her away. "Go. I'll take care of this other thing. Get us started on it."

Tim swung his head from Lucie to Joey and back. "Are you in the middle of something?"

She sure was. She just couldn't tell her cop boyfriend. He didn't appreciate her side investigations—even if, in her own craptastic way, she had a decent close rate.

Nope. What Tim wanted was a girlfriend who let the police do their jobs. Which was all fine and dandy and perfectly agreeable. Except when Lucie's BFF was in the slammer.

"No," Lucie assured him. "We're fine. Just business."

Sort of.

Tim cocked his head. "You know, one of the things I love about you is your sense of integrity. I mean, you wear your heart on your sleeve."

Awww, how sweet was he? "Well, thank you."

"You're welcome. There's a downside though."

"Downside?"

He tweaked her nose. "I always know when you're lying."

Joey smacked his hands together. "I'm out. Let's go, Ma, I'll drive you home."

"I want to walk."

"It's cold out. You're not walking. Plus, it'll be dark soon."

"Joseph, it's three o'clock. If I leave now, I'll be home by 3:15."

But Joey, being insanely protective, wouldn't tolerate that. "Come on, Ma. Get in the car."

He walked out front and hollered something. Probably to one of the guys in front of Petey's. This was their version of an intercom. Screaming from two storefronts away.

Mom and Lucie exchanged a look. "Just do it," Lucie said. "He's worked up about Ro and this is not a battle worth fighting. Plus, Dad is down at Petey's and he'll probably side with Joey. I don't have it in me to mediate tonight."

Mom snatched up her purse. "We need Roseanne out of prison. I can't live my life like this."

"She's not in *prison*. She's in jail."

Semantics maybe, but Lucie had spent a good portion of her lifetime compartmentalizing her issues regarding her father's choice of vocation. Prison meant convicted. Jail meant innocent until proven guilty and awaiting trial.

Big difference.

Mom marched toward the door. "If you need me, I'll be at home. With the barbarians. Tim, take my baby out for a nice dinner and make her smile."

Oh, boy. That smiling line brought a grin to the good detective's face. A spark of lust fired inside Lucie.

She and Tim? Good together.

In many ways.

Mom left, taking all the crazy Rizzo energy with her. Finally, some peace.

"So," Tim said, "want to tell me what was going on when I walked in here?"

Lucie dropped into her chair and tapped the mouse on her laptop. "I just have a few things to do before I close up. Is that okay?"

"Nice try. Spill."

"What? We were talking about Coitus."

And, oh my god, they needed a nickname for that dog.

Tim laughed. "Luce, I know you. And there is no way you're going to let Roseanne sit in a jail cell without helping. Please tell me you're not interfering in this investigation?"

She clicked the refresh button on her emails. Then hit it again just to give herself something to do while figuring out how to avoid this conversation with Tim.

"Shit," he said.

"I'm not interfering." She bit her lip. "Much."

Why couldn't she have been born a good liar?

"Shit."

"It's not that bad. I went to see Buzzy's sister."

Lucie gave up on watching her emails load and finally looked up at him. Her fair-skinned Irish boy's face flooded with color so fast his freckles should have popped off.

"Don't get mad," she said. "It was a business call. I thought, given the situation, I should reach out and see if we could settle the issue with Buzzy stealing our designs."

And to find out if Buzzy's agent might be a killer.

"Luce, I know what you're doing."

"What am I doing?"

Tim cocked an eyebrow. "You're hiding your investigation behind a business meeting."

"I'm trying to figure out what happened. Ro had a meeting with Frampton's that afternoon. She left here before 3:00. I have a call into the buyer there. Two calls actually. But she's not getting back to me."

"Can you blame her? Your employee just got arrested."

Lucie's worst nightmare. Only she always assumed any shunning would come from her father's bad behavior.

Not from Ro's.

But she didn't believe for a second that Ro was a murderer. Hot-headed at times, yes. Determined, most definitely. "All she did," Lucie said, "was send a tweet. That's it. How can they even pin a murder on her for that?"

CERTAIN QUESTIONS, TIM COULDN'T RESPOND TO. THIS WOULD be one of them. Even if he knew the answer, he couldn't comment on an active case.

Lucie knew that. All the Rizzos did.

The bells on the shop door jangled and Joey entered, his lips pressed into a tight line.

Lucie's head snapped back. "I thought you were taking Mom home."

"I got a call on the way, so I dropped her off and came back."

Crap. Based on Joey's body language, probably not good news. On cue, Joey made eye contact with Tim and there was nothing friendly about it.

The Rizzos, Tim had learned, were a loyal bunch. Nutty to the point of psychosis, but they stood by each other.

Ro's incarceration and the way they'd rallied around her proved it. It also put Tim, the cop, on the outs. Didn't matter that he loved Lucie. The breach between the Chicago PD and the Rizzos ran deep. Tim had known from his first date with Lucie that he'd have to find his place in the middle and get comfortable there.

So far, he and Lucie had managed sometimes being on opposite sides. They usually talked it through, respected each other's viewpoints, and agreed to disagree on certain things. This time? As sure as he was standing here, he knew he was boxed out.

Joey stopped about a foot from them, his pissy gaze shooting from Lucie to Tim and finally landing on Lucie.

He waggled his thumb in Tim's direction. "Did he tell you?"

"Tell me what?"

"About the witness?"

Witness?

"What witness?" Lucie asked.

"Joey," Tim said, "what the hell are you talking about?"

Joey hit him with a scathing look. "You're gonna tell me you don't know?"

Up to this point, Tim had never had a beef with Joey. For

the most part, they stayed out of each other's way and had even formed a halfway decent friendship. That said a lot, considering Lucie and Joey's closest friend had dated for four years.

One thing Tim and Joey had in common was a mile-wide protective streak. When it came to the women they loved, they agreed on the need to keep them safe.

And now Joey was pissed. Something that absolutely lacked a woo-hoo factor, but Tim's stones were just as rock solid as Joey's.

Tim met his stare. "Why don't you explain? Then I'll tell you if I know."

"Yes," Lucie said, her voice vibrating, riding the edge of control. "What witness?"

"Willie just called. Some woman saw Ro walking into Buzzy's around the time of the murder."

In the words of Tim's highly-experienced-in-the-world-of-law-enforcement grandfather: *Oh, shit.*

Lucie peered up at him, her big blue eyes stricken. *No. Nuh, nuh, nuh.*

Tim held up a hand. "Don't get ahead of yourself. I haven't heard this. Had no idea."

That alone frosted him. Another reminder of his boss's attempt to isolate him from a big case.

The gossip mill ran strong, though, and Tim heard the security video from the night of the murder had been deleted from the victim's hard drive. Whoever deleted the file didn't count on detectives getting a warrant that entitled them to copies of the security company's backups. But Tim couldn't talk about that. And the Rizzos would need to accept it.

"Right," Joey said, taking a step forward, getting up in Tim's grill. "You're always the guy not wanting to get involved. You probably didn't know about the security tapes either."

Tim stayed silent.

Lucie's eyes got big again. "What tapes?"

Joey waved one hand. "That problem with the security video from Buzzy's? They don't think it was turned off. They just can't find anything from the night Buzzy got killed."

"Come on," Lucie said.

"Relax, they're getting a warrant for the security company's records. They want to see what kind of activity the system had." Joey turned a hard glare on Tim. "You're telling me, with the hype about this case, you didn't know. You think I believe that?"

Tim stood stock still. If Joey Rizzo wanted to throw hands, they'd throw hands. No problem there. "I don't care what you believe. I care what your sister believes."

After a long few seconds, Joey backed off, literally retreating a step. Beside him, Lucie, still wore that bombed out look of a woman skeptical of her surroundings. Whatever Tim said next would stay with her. She was good that way. Honesty, she'd support. No matter what.

Neither of them had ever been afraid of the truth.

"Luce," he said, "some lines I don't cross. I've never lied to you. I've told you I can't comment. You know that means I have information I can't share. Whoever this witness is, I haven't heard about it. If I had, I'd stand here and tell you I can't comment. If I *had* known, I would have warned you something big was coming. I'd have prepared you. I would *not* let you be blindsided. When would I ever do that to you?"

10

———————

Lucie's feet wouldn't budge. How ironic that she should be standing in between her brother and Tim. Stuck between Rizzo world and law enforcement.

Looking into Tim's eyes though, she believed him. He'd never been a liar. His need for brutal honesty wouldn't allow it. Heck, sometimes she might prefer a lie. Like now, when she wanted to pretend this mess didn't exist.

"Never," she said. "You'd never do that to me."

"Thank you."

"You're welcome." She shifted to Joey. "This *witness* is either mistaken or she's lying."

"Well, she picked Ro out of a photo lineup."

"Then they need to do an in-person lineup. Photos can be tricky."

Tim shook his head. "We don't do those anymore. We show the witness six photos. One is usually our suspect."

Lucie swung her hands wide. "Well, that explains it. I'm sure the witness saw some other brunette going into that house. And, how do we know the police didn't put just one brunette—Ro—in their photo lineup?"

Again, Tim shook his head and Lucie wanted to throttle him.

"Typically, we put photos of similar looking people. It should have been all long-haired brunettes in the pack."

Lucie waved that off. "Yada, yada. I still don't believe it. I need to talk to her."

"Ro?" Joey said.

"Yes, Ro. Who do you think?"

She pressed two fingers into her forehead and squeezed her eyes closed. If she got through this without inflicting bodily harm on someone it would be a miracle. *Relax. One step at a time.*

A second later she dropped her hand and looked up at Tim. "My application for visiting privileges hasn't been approved yet. I know I can't call. How do I talk to Ro?"

Tim cocked his head one way, then the other. If she knew this man at all, he had an idea.

He headed for the door, waving his keys. "Lock up and let's go."

"Where?"

He swung the office door open. "If you want to see her, then move it. I'll get you in there. Or at least try."

That's all Joey needed to hear, because he hauled to the door. "I'm coming."

"Fine, but I can't get both of you in. Decide who's going in. The other waits. That's the best I can do."

Lucie gripped his arm. "Thank you. I know this is asking a lot."

"You didn't ask. I offered."

"Luce," Joey said, "you go in. I don't know if I can stand seeing her in that place. Temporary holding is one thing. An actual jail? That'd make me insane. Tell her I love her."

Her brother. Total mush. At least right now. In ten

minutes he'd be a jerk and she'd forget the whole thing. But for now? How sweet was he? "Aw, Joey." Lucie went up on tip-toes and kissed his cheek. "You're a good guy."

"Yeah, well, don't spread it around. I got a reputation to protect."

TIM DID HIS MAGIC, FLASHING HIS BADGE AND MAKING NICE with the guard at the main entrance to the Cook County Jail's women's division. According to the information board, the two-story building contained sixteen wings and held over 700 female inmates of all security levels. Lucie's lungs froze over the idea of Ro mixed in with lowlife murderers. Well, maybe she shouldn't judge the lowlifes since currently Ro was considered one of them.

To think, she'd had enough of jails when her father had been incarcerated. How did the Rizzos always wind up back where they started?

Tim shook hands with the guard, stowed his badge in his suit pocket, and waved Lucie over.

"We're in," he said, keeping his voice low.

Tim O'Brien. What a guy. "Thank you."

"You only have fifteen minutes. While they're bringing her to a room, figure out what you want to say. I don't know how long your application will take, so make use of this time. She can always call you."

"Those calls are recorded."

"Yes, they are. Like I said, make use of your time, Luce. I can only go so far."

She knew that. He'd taken a huge risk with this. For her. If his boss found out he'd used his badge to sneak Lucie into the jail, it would cause problems. Or maybe cops did things like this. Who knew? Tim certainly never shared that information with her.

"I really do appreciate this."

"I..." He shook his head.

"What?"

He checked the guard's position, making sure they were out of earshot. "I don't want my job being a thing between us. Joey and your dad operate a certain way. The cops they know are willing to risk their jobs by leaking info. I'm not doing it. If I can help, I will. Otherwise, my work is off limits."

Lucie nodded. "I'm sorry. They're just used to...something different."

"Meaning they don't like cops telling them no."

"Exactly."

"Well, too bad." The guard waved Lucie through the x-ray machine and Tim followed behind. "I'll wait out here."

"You can come in. It's okay."

"No. It's better this way. It'll give you two a few minutes. If you need me, holler for the guard."

The guard led Lucie down a long corridor to a set of steel doors with a lone window. He stopped at the door and tipped his head up to the camera mounted above the wall. A second later, a loud buzz echoed through the cement hallway followed by the clunk of a disengaging lock.

Once inside, they navigated another maze of hallways and doors. By the time they reached the final door, Lucie was all turned around. She wouldn't have been able to find her way out with a compass.

Which, she supposed, was the point in a jail.

Another buzz sounded and the guard pushed the door open. Inside the tiny white-walled room sat Ro, her hands cuffed to a hook on the shiny metal table and her feet shackled. Trussed up like a wild animal. Fierce, paralyzing anger punched Lucie in the solar plexus. She paused, breathing in the stale air. She didn't have time for a fit right now.

Later.

Now she had fifteen minutes to get her friend cleared of a murder charge.

She rushed to the table, ready to throw her arms around Ro.

"No contact," the guard said. "Everything is on video."

Lucie drew up short. "Okay. Right. I'm sorry."

The guard nodded. "Fifteen minutes. I'm right outside this door."

As if Ro, the big bad murderer, could break a rule when shackled like a wild animal.

The door closed and Ro shook her head. "Oh. My. God. Are they kidding me with these shackles?"

"I think it's protocol." Lucie hurried into the chair and set her hands on the table, itching to touch the woman who'd been her best friend for twenty years. If nothing else, to let her know that everything would be okay.

Can't.

A total first in the Lucie-Ro saga. If Lucie needed further proof of the unfolding nightmare, it was found in Ro's ensemble of baggy prison scrubs. Her long hair was pulled into a loose ponytail. In her lifetime, Lucie had maybe seen Ro without makeup ten times. Not that Ro needed makeup or was afraid to be seen without it. She simply liked "putting herself together" before leaving the house.

Now, seeing her skin scrubbed clean and way too pale, accentuating the dark circles under her eyes, the reality of their situation became a full-throttle nightmare.

Luce glanced up at the camera. "I don't think they can

hear us. Tim said it's just video. Are you okay? I mean, aside from being in here?"

"I'm fine. Willie got me moved out of the high security wing. Now I'm in with the gals in minimum security. At least I won't get jumped in the shower. With any luck. And, hey, my cellmate moved out this morning."

A private cell. Excellent.

"Good. Hopefully it'll stay that way until we get you out. Joey is outside. I think he was afraid he'd freak if he came in here. He said to...um...tell you that he loved you."

The corners of Ro's mouth tilted up. A quasi-smile that was anything but happy. "I know he's a jerk sometimes, but he really is a big softie. Tell him I love him too. And, honestly, I don't want him seeing me like this. It's...embarrassing. I mean, I can't even put a face on."

Before her BFF got on a roll, Lucie held her hands up. "We don't have a lot of time. If we're going to get you out of here, you have to tell me about this witness identifying you. Ro, please, tell me you didn't go to Buzzy's that day."

She scrunched her nose and Lucie's stomach twisted.

Oh no.

"Come on," Lucie said, her voice loud and echoing in the bland room.

The door swung open and the guard popped his head in. "Problem?"

Lucie and Ro both looked over at him. "No sir," Ro said.

"No, sir," Lucie repeated. "Sorry. My bad."

After a perfunctory nod, the guard disappeared again.

"I'm sorry," Ro said. "After you caught me tweeting at her, I didn't want to get in trouble again. I felt bad about the idea of a lawsuit, and I thought if Buzzy and I could talk, maybe we'd settle it. I left Frampton's and went to her house." Ro made a move to grab Lucie's hand, but the cuffs held her in place. "No touching. Right. Anyway, you've worked so hard and I didn't want some crazy lawsuit stressing you out. You know me, I wanted to fix it. And maybe beat her up for dissing us. But I *didn't*. Luce, I swear to you, I didn't do it."

She went to Buzzy's. On the day the woman was murdered.

Damn it.

Okay. They'd just work the problem. That's all. No histrionics. No panic. No arguing. *I've got this.*

"So you went there. What happened?"

"Nothing happened. I knocked on the door and rang the bell, but she didn't answer. All I heard was that crazy bird squawking from inside. I swear that thing is stone-cold nuts."

No kidding there.

"And then what?"

Ro shrugged. "Nothing. I left."

"What time was that?"

"Maybe about 4:30."

Shoot. Buzzy was found soon after, because it had been on the evening news. "Where does this witness come in?"

"It has to be the woman who was walking her dog. After Buzzy didn't answer, I left. I got just outside the front gate and the woman was passing. Luce, she had the most adorable Pomeranian, but that sweet baby needed some bling. As soon as I'm out of here, we're doing an entire line for toy dogs. I can see it all now. Pinks and purples and diamonds. It'll be *fabulous*."

"What's it going to take to get you focused here? You're all over the place and the clock is ticking."

"Sorry. But that's it. I told the woman she had an adorable dog and I left. I went straight to your mom's house from there to talk some sense into that idiot brother of yours."

Lucie thought back. When Ro had walked into Mom's that night, she'd come straight from Buzzy's. Which meant...

"Oh, Ro."

"What?"

"I got the text about Buzzy right after you walked into Mom's. We hadn't even had dinner. How long did it take you to get there?"

"Well, I will say the traffic was filthy that night. Some dumbass rear-ended a bus and caused a pileup that turned into a mess on the Kennedy. Total shut down. It had to have taken me at least an hour. Probably longer. If I had my phone, I could tell you."

"Why?"

"I was answering my emails while sitting in traffic."

"You are a complete menace. You're going to kill someone if you don't stop with that." Bad word choice. Lucie waved it away. "Whatever. So, ninety minutes in the car. If it hit the news in that timeframe it means one of two things."

Ro scrunched her nose. Yep, she was starting to grasp it.

Lucie tapped her hands on the metal table. "Are you picking up what I'm putting down here?"

"Buzzy was killed after I left."

"Or, she was already dead when you were banging on her door."

AT 7:00 A.M. THE FOLLOWING MORNING, LUCIE ENTERED THE front door of Coco Barknell, the doggie bells welcoming her into creepy morning darkness. Even with the sun about to pop up, the office remained shrouded. Something niggled at the back of Lucie's neck.

The silence didn't help.

Call it hyper-sensitivity—or paranoia—from growing up with a father who always sat with his back to the wall to thwart assassins, but something felt...off.

Maybe she simply wasn't used to being alone in the office. Definite possibility since Ro liked to arrive first and get the coffee going.

Whatever the reason, timers for the lights might be a good idea. With Ro otherwise occupied, Lucie would be logging extra hours before the fashion show next week. She didn't want to be walking into creepy darkness every morning.

Lucie smacked the light switch just inside the entrance and the room flooded with light.

"Whoa."

The niggling at the back of her neck exploded, sending her heart into an erratic slam against her chest. Her gaze shot to the garment rack where, just last night, Ro's samples had been meticulously hung and organized.

The rack was empty, its contents strewn about on the floor. Buttons, rhinestones—even the silly crocheted flowers Mom had sewn on a sweater—all scattered amongst the shredded fabric.

Lucie stepped back, ready to run. Ready to flee this place she'd put so much energy into.

A fierce stab of anger gripped her, kept her rooted in her spot. Someone had broken in and destroyed every one of Ro's samples. Every. One.

That pissed Lucie off.

Big time.

The bells on the door jangled and in walked Dad and

Joey, wheeling the giant rolling whiteboard one of the guys at Petey's had borrowed three weeks ago. What they were doing down at Petey's that required a white board, Lucie hadn't asked.

In truth, she didn't want to know. Denial was sometimes a girl's best friend. Where was denial now? When she really needed it.

"Move it," Joey said. "You're in the way."

Her father's mouth pressed into a hard line. "What the hell's this mess?"

"Someone broke in. Last night. Those are all Ro's designs. Destroyed."

"Dad, stay with Lucie." Joey sidestepped the mess, beelining for the back of the shop.

Dad swung the white board parallel to the door and drew her in front of it, using it as a shield from anyone peeping in.

As crazy as her dad made her, these were the moments that brought her back to childhood. Back to being six years old and worshipping the protective father who made sure his kids were safe. The one who held her hand at the carnival and took her on carousels because he refused to let her out of his sight.

Joey popped out of the storeroom and checked the bathroom, flipping on the light, and then proceeding to the break room.

"All clear," he said. "They broke out the window in the back."

That damned window. She'd already had one incident with someone climbing through it and now this. She might have to board that thing up. Ro would have a fit over it being an eyesore, but if it kept intruders out, Lucie would do it.

She stared down at the floor, her gaze flicking over the

mess. Poor Ro. "Joey, we can't tell her about this. Ro. She'll be devastated. I'll see if Mom can recreate them."

"She'll do it," he said. "She won't want to hear the screaming when Ro gets out."

Good point.

Joey circled one finger. "Did you touch anything?"

Evidence. They'd need to preserve it. Lucie stepped back, away from the shredded scraps barely a foot in front of her. "Just the door."

"Good," Dad said. "Let's hope the feds are still watching me."

How did everything manage to become about her father? She whirled on him. "Dad, please. This isn't about you."

Dad angled his head in that way that instilled fear from the time she and Joey were toddlers. When he did that head thing, it meant something. Something ugly and mean. And scary.

"About *me*?" he said. "You watch your mouth. I'm not talking about me. I'm talking about the federal agents who watch Petey's from all sides. This is one time surveillance might do us some good. I'll take the feds breakfast and see if they saw anybody nosing around."

Shame bubbled in Lucie's stomach. For all his faults, her father meant well. She stepped toward him, grabbed his forearms and squeezed. "Dad, I'm so sorry. I didn't mean that. I swear. Please, I didn't mean it."

"Blah, blah," Joey said. "Get over yourself. We need to call the cops. And Dad's right, maybe the feds saw someone coming in here."

Maybe.

Lucie let go of her father and turned back to the mess littering her floor. One thing was for sure. Whoever did this, didn't want those samples to be of any use. This was personal. A total invasion. The destruction of something Ro had painstakingly designed. Hours of work, destroyed.

And Lucie didn't believe the timing was coincidental. Not when she'd been nosing around about Buzzy's murder.

"Luce," Joey said, "someone isn't happy with you."

She shook her head. "For once, I agree with you. But that's too bad. I'm not stopping until Ro is free."

11

<hr>

Two hours later, the Franklin PD had processed the scene and cleared out, leaving Lucie, Dad and Joey to sweep up the mess on the floor. All of it eating away at her carefully crafted schedule.

"Too bad there wasn't any blood or something on this stuff," Joey said. "At least then they'd have taken it as evidence and saved us a shit-ton of work."

Her brother. Always keeping his priorities straight.

Lucie didn't even have a snappy comeback. In one way, Joey had a point. The lack of blood or any other identifiable substance meant the crime scene guys simply photographed the scene, leaving the contents. Which meant, nothing about the mess would help them find the perp, as Tim liked to say.

Tim. She'd have to call him. Let him know about the break-in. Only, she couldn't do it now. He'd come running over and the presence of her detective boyfriend would interfere with her meeting. A meeting he wouldn't approve of. In his mind, bumping up the activity in her investigation meant opening herself up to danger.

Well, she'd risk it.

And Tim couldn't know about it. Simple as that. She'd have her meeting and call him on her way downtown.

Joey scooped handfuls of fabric, dumping them in a trash bag as a fresh bout of anger seared Lucie's midsection. Bastards. Whoever they were, she couldn't let them get away with it.

"Baby girl, where do you want this?"

Dad stood beside the white board he and Joey had wheeled back to the shop. She pointed at Ro's desk. "Put it there."

Where she didn't have to look at Ro's empty desk. Without Ro the place felt...vacant. Lonely. If Lucie was the brains behind the operation, Ro was the fearless muscle. No matter what the task, she always took it on.

And now Lucie couldn't imagine running the business without her.

Enter the whiteboard and her meeting.

"The Cock Heads will be here any time."

Joey waved Dad away and positioned the white board in front of Ro's desk. "You invited the Dick Heads?"

Lucie grunted. After the morning they'd had, he wanted to start? "I've told you a hundred times. Don't call them Dick Heads."

Dad dropped into one of the conference table chairs. "Ho, with the language." He pulled his phone out and stared at the screen as if an alien possessed it. "I hate this phone. Why can't I go back to the other one?"

"Because it's a flip phone," Joey said.

"And what?"

Lucie shook her head. "The *Cock* Heads are my friends. And Ro's. They wanted to help. They know a lot of people in this town. By the way, after this meeting, I need your help."

"What else is new?"

Always complaining about his growing role in the busi-ness, Joey had never once let her down. Secretly, she knew he liked spending time with the dogs.

"With Ro...unavailable, I need to pick up the slack. We have a dress rehearsal for the fashion show today. Which means, you have to do a couple of extra walks."

"Otis?"

"No. He's with me at the show. The swim trunks didn't fit so we're trying him in our new plus-sized line. "

"You know, I didn't want to say anything, but I think he resents that."

"Otis?"

"Yeah. He's not fat. He's beefy. Bulldogs are supposed to be beefy."

Beefy. Right. "Joey, I said the same thing, but, honestly, I'm not sure Otis really understands what plus-sized means."

"Believe me, he understands."

Lucie snorted. "You're a big mush."

The door opened and in walked Jimmy Two-Toes and Lemon, two of Dad's cronies from Petey's. The two of them were carbon copies of her father. Dress pants, dress shirt, no tie and perfectly groomed hair. Lemon may have been the shorter, lighter haired one of the bunch, but he refused to be outdone in the fashion department.

"Hey, Luce," Lemon said. "We're here for the meeting."

Lucie gave Joey the hairy eyeball.

"Hey," he said, "they were at Petey's and asked where the white board went."

Since when did mob guys get up so early?

At this point, if it meant getting Ro out of jail, all hands on deck. Plus, Jimmy and Lemon did have a lot of contacts.

"Thanks, guys," Lucie said. "Have a seat. There's coffee in

the back if you want. I can't guarantee it's any good though. Ro is the coffee lady around here."

The two of them disappeared into the back room. Joey took a seat next to Dad and was immediately handed the alien phone. "I think I got a text. How do I know?"

"Do you know anyone who knows how to text?"

"Probably not."

"Then what are you worried about?"

"Good point."

The doggie bells on the door flew again. Cock Head Ben rushed through, holding the door open for Kristy and Annabelle.

"Sorry we're late," Annabelle said, gently removing her fedora so she wouldn't disturb the feathers.

Annabelle, aka the Cock Heads' resident hostess with the mostest, always donned some sort of peacock headwear.

"No problem," Lucie said. "I appreciate you guys coming so early."

This was friendship. Two of the three of them were on their way to work, but they'd agreed to come to the meeting if it meant helping Ro.

As nutty as these people were, they loved Lucie—and Ro—and Lucie was proud to call them her friends.

Annabelle wrapped her in a tight hug and the usual scent of her cranberry lotion knocked Lucie's stress level down a notch. Finally, something normal. Even if it was only body lotion.

"I'm so sorry about Ro," Annabelle said. "We all are."

"Thank you. But we're going to prove her innocent. I know we are."

Lucie waved everyone to the table. "Cock Heads, I think you know my brother, Joey, but this is my dad."

Hellos were exchanged along with that ever-present awe

over meeting the notorious Joe Rizzo. What Lucie couldn't tell was whether it was good awe or bad awe. People either loved Dad or hated him. Not him, per se, but his lifestyle. In actuality, Dad was a nice guy. Always willing to help or give money to the homeless. He kept it quiet, but every morning he'd buy a dozen breakfast sandwiches and take them three blocks down to the old warehouse where a bunch of homeless guys slept.

Call it the dichotomy of Dad. Criminal who'd most likely done unspeakable things versus supporter of the homeless.

Jimmy and Lemon returned from their coffee run and more introductions were made. Lucie gave everyone a minute to assemble, then grabbed a marker from the little shelf on the white board.

Ben, a corporate lawyer, sat forward. "What about Ro? Update us."

"Nothing new aside from what I told you. They denied bail and now there's a witness who saw Ro at the scene. It's just insanity."

"Alibi?"

"I'm working on that. The police confiscated her computer and most of her files, but I have a call into the buyer at Frampton's. Ro had a meeting with her right before Buzzy died. I'm hoping the buyer can provide the alibi. For all I know, the police have already talked to her, so I'm not sure."

Ben made a humming noise. "Well, they went after Ro for a reason."

Yes, they did. Lucie nodded. "Twitter smack down with Buzzy."

"Oh, no," Annabelle said. "That social media is a snake pit."

Ben, suddenly the Cock Head's version of Perry Mason,

circled one hand. "Tell me about this smack down. Why were they fighting?"

"Buzzy, God rest her soul, stole a few of Ro's designs. The ones for the fashion show."

Kristy gasped. "Not the ones you showed us last week."

"Yep. She's already selling them on her website."

"I hope you're suing her ass," Jimmy said.

"God rest her soul," Annabelle said.

"I'm trying to work it out before it gets to that. My lawyer is working on it."

At the end of the table Kristy, a shy, recent college grad raised her hand. "I heard that Buzzy is—*was*—a real...um..."

Joey rolled his eyes. "Let me help you. She was a real bitch."

The room erupted into a series of gasps and "God rest her souls." Lucie sighed. "Everyone, please, pipe down. I want to hear this."

"I don't know specifics, but a couple of months ago there was something on the news about Buzzy firing her agent."

"I spoke to Lorraine yesterday—she's Buzzy's sister—and she told me the agent wasn't in the picture anymore. But it's a lead."

Lucie turned to the white board and jotted *AGENT* before turning back to her crack team.

"Okay, gang. I visited Roseanne last night. She's doing okay, but we need to get organized here. With the witness coming forward, things are moving fast and I'm not sure the police are still looking for the real killer."

"Where's Tim?" Dad wanted to know.

"No Tim," Lucie said.

She hated keeping secrets from him. As much as he told her to stay out of it, he knew better. She couldn't let a loved one rot in jail.

Well, not if they were innocent.

That didn't mean dragging Tim into this though. He'd helped her last night, but that was his idea.

"He should be here," Dad said. "He can help."

Lucie let out a sigh. "No Tim. If there's something I think he can help with, I'll ask him. Otherwise, we're doing this our way." Before he could argue, she turned to the Cock Heads. "Here's what we know so far. This witness is legit."

Annabelle's mouth flopped open and Lucie shot her hand up. "Don't freak. Ro did go to Buzzy's house. She knocked on the door and rang the bell, but no one answered. She never went inside. She left and ran into one of the neighbors on the sidewalk. That's it."

"What time was this?"

Lucie turned back to the whiteboard. "About 4:30." She drew a front door and added *4:30 PM* under it. "She got to my mom's around 6:00." She added that to her timeline. "Either Buzzy was already dead at 4:30 or—"

Annabelle gasped. What was with the gasping?

"Or," Lucie continued, "the killer was inside with her."

"Oh, *no*," Kristy said.

"Yeah. Terrible thought. I could be wrong."

"The timing fits," Joey said. "Let's go with that theory. Besides the agent, who are we looking at suspect-wise?"

Kristy raised her hand and Lucie waved her marker at her. "You don't have to raise your hand."

"Okay. Thank you. If Buzzy wasn't a nice person, it could be anyone. Has she stolen other ideas? Or maybe someone who worked for her?"

Dad waggled two fingers. "Put me and Jimmy and Lemon on that board. We'll talk to a couple of cops. See who they're looking at."

Okay. Now they were cooking.

Lucie added her name to the board. "I'll come up with some reason to talk to Buzzy's sister again. And," she spun back to Joey. "Since I'll have the Ninja Bitches with me after the fashion show dress rehearsal, I'll swing by Buzzy's neighborhood and walk the dogs. Maybe I'll see something."

"They won't let you in," Dad said. "They still have the street barricaded."

"Yes, but if I'm a neighbor, they have to let me in."

He rolled his bottom lip out. "How are you gonna pull that off?"

"I have no idea."

NINJA BITCHES IN TOW, LUCIE NABBED A PARKING SPACE THREE blocks over from Buzzy's, grabbed her tote bag off the passenger seat floor, and pulled out her blond wig and floppy winter hat.

Frankie had always had a thing for that wig. At first, he'd hated it because, at that time, she'd been forced to fend off dogjackers by going incognito. After that? It was all twisted stripper fantasies. She laughed at the memory. Sometimes she simply needed a kindred spirit to commiserate with. By virtue of his biology, Frankie understood the insanity of being a mob kid. The *life*. He knew all about the mix of emotions. Anger, embarrassment, fear, how all of it coiled together and made her mind race.

In the backseat, Fannie, one half of the adorable and fearless Shih-Tzu duo, let out a happy yip. Josie and Fannie lived in a ritzy neighborhood, so they'd feel right at home with the aroma of oodles of money. They both still wore the trench coats and belts Lucie had put them in for the fashion show rehearsal. She might as well road test the coats to see if they'd actually be usable or if they were simply doggie haute couture.

Two birds. One stone. That was Lucie.

She slipped her wig and hat on, brushed out the ends and called it a done deal. Then she pointed a finger between Josie and Fannie.

"Now look, I'm sorry to drag you girls into this, but I need props and you're two of the cutest darned props going. If we get caught, it's on me. Don't feel bad. Okay?"

The two of them looked at each other and—wait—did Josie's shoulder just twitch?

A Ninja Bitch shrug.

Lucie wouldn't have been surprised. These dogs really did think they were human.

Lucie hopped out and opened the back door. She'd strapped the girls into their car harnesses and took the opportunity to snap the leash on Fannie. She didn't need one of them busting loose and getting lost.

"Okay, girls, let's do this. Lucie and the bitches ride again."

The girls jumped from the backseat and immediately rushed to a giant oak tree, where they both let out a stream of urine that could sink a destroyer.

How did such little dogs hold that much?

The girls finished their business and Lucie led them one block south toward Buzzy's. These streets, with their elegant brownstones and squeaky-clean sidewalks, could have been interchangeable. The homes all held their own appeal, but most had been refaced, if not torn down altogether and rebuilt, so the newness, although beautiful, robbed the old-world comfort from the area.

But, she wasn't shopping for a house. No sir. If her plan worked, she'd be a resident. Heh, heh, heh.

She cut down the block that backed up to Buzzy's and counted down the number of houses. At the third home—*no gate, yay*—phase one of Lucie's plan took hold.

"Okay, girls, look natural. Pretend we belong here."

The girls paused, looked up at her then at each other, and scampered off to another tree. The detour gave Lucie ample opportunity to scope out the alley beside the home. These dogs. Perfect accomplices.

Josie chose that moment to poop. On a normal day, Lucie would be thrilled. Right now? Not so much. She whipped out a poop bag, but waited a few seconds. Usually, when one pooped the other followed. Lucie swore it was some sort of competitive thing between them.

And...yep, as soon as Josie stepped away from her mess, Fannie squared up.

If nothing else, these trench coats were getting the full workup today. Both dogs had peed and pooped and, so far, not a stain to be seen. Excellent craftsmanship from the Coco Barknell team.

Lucie dealt with the dueling poop explosion and tied the baggie around the leash to keep her hands free until they found a garbage can. She casually scanned the area, found it blissfully quiet and took a breath.

"Here we go, girls."

She led the dogs down the alley separating the second and third houses. If her plan worked, she'd cut across the yards that backed up to each other and come out on the next block.

When at Buzzy's the prior week, after circling the block, she'd noticed a realtor's sign on the home behind Buzzy's. The house still had the outside lights on. In the middle of the day. No one inside? Couldn't count on that. Mom forgot to turn their porch light off on a regular basis.

Still, as she cruised through the yard she glanced back and found the curtain raised on the French door. Bare kitchen. The owners had already moved out.

Even better.

Fannie, bless her alpha soul, led the charge through the alley and Lucie let her go. Now wasn't the time to correct her bad leash behaviors.

Just ahead, the mouth of the dark alley separating Buzzy's home from the neighbor's—Lorraine's house, thankfully, was the one on the other side—opened to streaming sunlight. The girls picked up their pace, itching to explore more trees.

The girls burst out of the alley, their little legs carrying them along as their nails tap, tap, tapped against the cement.

"Okay, girls, slow down."

Just as Lucie cleared the alley, someone yelled.

Dang it. Not even to the sidewalk yet.

"Hey, lady!"

She glanced over. A uniformed cop stood at the corner behind a barricade. Refusing to leave his post, he waved her over.

Not a big deal. She'd expected some variation of this. Just not so soon.

"Good morning, officer."

"Yeah, good morning. What are you doing?"

Lucie drew her eyebrows together, feigning confusion. "Um, I'm walking my dogs."

"Not here you're not. We need to keep this block clear."

"But," she pointed behind her, "the house behind this one is mine. Well, it's not mine yet. We close tomorrow. I'm just so excited and I wanted to give the girls a tour of their new neighborhood. Say hello girls."

The girls plopped their butts down and growled. And they wondered why the crazy neighbor saddled them with the Ninja Bitches moniker?

The cop stepped back.

"Oh, just ignore them. They're protective. Anyway, I thought I'd show them the area and see if I could meet some of the neighbors."

"It's not a good time for that. We got all kinds of nutcases out here."

"Hey," another officer yelled from the opposite side of the street.

Obviously curious, he wandered to the middle of the block. Something about him was familiar. The big shouldered, linebacker build.

Uh-oh.

Lucie dipped her head, hoping the floppy hat would hide her face.

"What's up?" the bigger cop said as he approached.

"I just found her walking her dogs. She says she owns the house behind this one."

Still with her head down, she slid a sideways glance at the second cop. *Crud.* The officer coming toward her was the seriously cute Lindstrom who'd helped when her dogs kept getting dogjacked last spring.

Given she hadn't seen or spoken to him in months, he might not remember her. The blond wig wouldn't hurt her chances.

Fannie let out another growl and Lucie took the opportunity to squat down, her back to Lindstrom. *Please, go away.*

"Lucie? Is that you? What's with the wig?"

Roll with it. As usual, her only luck was bad. But, heck, she'd been in worse predicaments than this. She stood, faced Lindstrom, and blinked a couple of times. Feigning surprise couldn't hurt.

She whipped off a big-butt smile. "Officer Lindstrom, how nice to see you."

The first cop did that bottom lip roll again. "You know each other?"

"Sort of," Lindstrom said. "I helped Ms. Rizzo on a case."

"Rizzo?"

"Yeah," Lindstrom said, "*that* Rizzo."

"Whoa. She said she just bought this house."

Lindstrom eyed her and Lucie played dumb, allowing the girls to pull her to the tree in front of Buzzy's house.

Lindstrom waggled his thumb at the first cop. "I got this."

The other cop marched back to his post. Lindstrom, feet planted, crossed his arms and stared at her with a mix of curiosity and concern.

"Why do I think you didn't just buy this house?"

"I can explain."

"This should be good."

"Hey. That's not nice."

Lindstrom laughed. "On the contrary. I'm preparing for the entertainment. In my dealings with you so far, you've given me great stories to tell."

He had her there.

Then he sobered, his blue eyes narrowing slightly. "Is this about your friend who got locked up?"

Lucie nodded. "It's not what you think though. I'm not trying to sneak into Buzzy's."

"Thank you, sweet Jesus. You were partners or something with her, right?"

"Yes." Lucie pointed at the trench coats. "A line of doggie clothes."

Lindstrom nodded his appreciation. "Nice. I like the belt."

"I know, right? *Anyway*, I thought maybe I could talk with some of the neighbors. Roseanne didn't kill her. I know it."

Lindstrom sighed. "Lucie, come on. You're killing me here. This is an active investigation."

"It's a public street."

"Which is currently barricaded."

"Not to residents."

"You can't knock on doors. No way."

Hmmm. Lindstrom was being a hardnose. Her history working for one of the city's top investment bankers had taught her a few things. The fine art of negotiation was one of them. Right now, she had to strike a deal with Lindstrom.

"But," she said, "I can walk along the sidewalk. The sidewalk is public."

"And?"

"And what? If I stay on the sidewalk, I'm not bothering anyone. Please. Just let me walk the dogs down this block and back up the other side. Then, I'll leave." She held a hand up. "I swear."

"No."

Last time she'd talked with Lindstrom, he'd been so accommodating. Now? Total roadblock. Time to pull out the big guns. "You know," she said, "there's a ton of press around here. My father came with me to Buzzy's the other day and, holy moly, that was a mess. He about caused a riot."

"Lucie?"

"Yes?"

"Are you threatening to unleash Joe Rizzo, media whore, on me?"

Her? Would she do that?

In a New York minute. She offered up a toothy smile. "Wouldn't it be so much easier if you just let me walk the block? I promise, after that, I'll leave."

The corner of his mouth quirked. "Or I could lock you up for trespassing."

"The media would love that."

Now he flat-out laughed. "Damn you."

"I'm sorry."

"No you're not."

His shoulders drooped and the itch of success bloomed inside Lucie. She might not have Ro's boobs to sway a man, but she knew how to make things happen without popping a button.

Again, she smiled. "I promise. One spin up and down the block and I'm gone."

He gazed up the street for a few long seconds, then turned the other way before coming back to her. "Go. Don't dawdle. Chances are, no one will leave their house."

"You could be right." She hoped not.

"One lap and you'll leave? I have your word?"

"Yes, sir. I promise."

Except if one of the neighbors comes out.

LINDSTROM WALKED BACK TO THE POLICE BARRICADE, BUT KEPT a hard eye on her while she strolled from tree to tree.

"Okay, Bitches," Lucie said to the girls. "You need to stall. Stop at every tree if you have to. Got it?"

Fannie looked up at her then went back to sniffing the ground. *Way to help a girl out, sister.*

Lucie's phone rang. A 312 number. Who could this be? She poked the screen. "Hello?"

"It's Lindstrom."

Lucie whipped back and he gave her a too-doo-loo wave. He'd saved her contact info from last spring?

"I know what you're doing," he said. "Quit screwing around and get out of here."

"You said one lap. I didn't realize there was a time limit."

"*I* didn't realize it would be a three-day lap."

A small delivery truck—one of those organic grocery services— whooshed to a stop at the curb.

This could be a lead.

"Gotta go." She hung up on Lindstrom.

The driver, a young guy about Lucie's age, wore a uniform of bright green pants, a white button down, and a green and white captain's hat. Poor guy. With that uniform, his company should get sued for employee abuse.

He opened the truck's back doors, grabbed two large sacks, and swung the doors closed again.

"Hi," Lucie said.

He stopped midstride. "Uh, hi."

"Making a delivery?"

"Yeah. Cute dogs."

Little did he know these *cute* girls could take his leg off. "Thanks. This is Josie and Fannie."

Fannie plopped her butt on the ground and Josie flipped to her back. Unable to resist, Lucie squatted and gave her a rub while the guy hustled to the house to make his delivery. No sense holding up someone's food order. When he returned? She'd pump him for intel.

She wandered to the tree next to his truck and the girls obliged by giving it a squirt.

A minute later, the driver jogged down the path. "So," Lucie said, "I'm new in the neighborhood. Do you have any brochures on your service?"

"Sure."

He snatched a brochure from his back pocket. How good was this guy carrying brochures in his pocket? Lucie should hire him to help with Coco Barknell marketing.

"We're an independent company." He pointed to the service's logo. "All the products are hand-picked by the owners. Their kids all have gluten or nut allergies."

"Oh, wow."

"Yeah. That's what's good about this. You order everything online and have it delivered. Especially if you have small kids. No dragging them out to the store and dealing with the insane parking around here. Do you live on the block?"

"Not yet. We'll be moving in soon. You're the regular driver?"

The kid nodded. "I handle the city."

No easy task. Being a dog walker and having experienced the challenge of getting from location to location, Lucie sympathized. She'd finally bought a couple of scooters for the staff to use.

He pointed to the house he'd just made a delivery to. "The Eppersons are regulars. I'd do the Eppersons and Ms. Sneider at the same time. It's weird to be here and not have a delivery for her."

"It's scary that something like this could happen in such a nice neighborhood."

"Just goes to show you. No one is safe."

There was a fatalist attitude. "I suppose," Lucie said.

"I have to say, I was surprised it was a woman who got arrested."

Do tell. "Really? Why?"

The guy shrugged. "I don't know. There was always this guy here when I delivered her orders. Since it happened in her house, I figured it was him that did it."

What guy? Buzzy wasn't married and, although Lucie wasn't exactly in-the-know about Buzzy's love life, the woman had never mentioned a significant other.

"Was he her boyfriend?"

The delivery guy shrugged. "He answered the door in a robe one morning."

A boyfriend. She'd need to research this. Maybe call Reece and see if Buzzy had a current love interest. Even if it was a causal relationship, the man needed to be investigated.

"Hey!"

Whoopsie. Lucie swung around and found the cop from the other end of the street bearing down on them.

"I gotta go," the driver said. "My boss will kill me if these cops shut me down."

"Go," Lucie said. "I don't want to get you in trouble."

"Thanks. And try us out. First order has free delivery."

She totally needed to hire this guy.

She held up the brochure. "Thanks. I'll give it a look."

Right along with the bathrobe-wearing mystery man.

12

Lucie stormed into Coco Barknell headquarters and unloaded her notes from her chat with the delivery guy. She'd have to start keeping a stash of extra notepads in her car. While scrambling to get her notes written, she'd run out of paper and wound up using any available writing surface. The grocery service brochure, napkins, an old envelope, the back of her insurance card, a receipt, a torn dry cleaning tag.

Now, all of it sat in a pile on her desk and she'd have to make sense of it before her meeting with the caterer in—wait for it—thirty minutes.

Being a type A personality, she didn't like mess. Of any kind. And for the last two days that seemed to be all she had. With Ro locked up, Lucie now handled the fashion show details, payroll, taxes, schedules and every other administrative function.

I've got this. She'd simply get a fresh notebook from Ro's stash of spirals in the supply closet and put everything related to the case in there. Getting organized was the first step. Then, when she had all her notes together, she'd talk to

Tim. Show him what she'd found and see if any of it would help Ro's case.

He wouldn't be happy about her butting into police business, but he'd understand.

Eventually.

After grabbing a notebook from the back, she plopped down at her desk and started sorting through the scraps of paper to transcribe.

The door swung open and in walked...Frankie.

Oh, God.

Frankie. Gorgeous, funny, smart, Frankie. Home.

Her mouth may have dropped open. She lifted her hand to check and, yep, there she sat, jaw hanging open, staring at her first love. After years of her begging him to move away from Franklin and their mobbed-up families, he'd decided to take a job in New York just as her business was taking off. And despite his asking her to move with him, she couldn't do it. She had responsibilities now. A business to run. Employees to support.

And now he was back, standing in her shop.

In the months he'd been gone, they'd exchanged a text or two, but that was it. No calls, no visits, nothing. Tim deserved her full attention and she'd given it to him. With Tim, there was no baggage. No familial pull. No expectations beyond their own.

Just her and her hunky Irish cop. The one increasingly frustrated with her putting him in awkward positions with his bosses.

Frankie.

Seeing him now, for the first time since he'd left, sent a jab of pain right to the center of her chest. It could have been the chili hot dog she'd eaten at lunch, but she doubted it.

He halted just inside the doorway and their eyes met for a few long seconds, all the words trapped somewhere between them. No man's land.

"Hi," he said, his voice hovering in the vast space between tentative and the normal Mr. Confident Frankie.

He shoved his hands in the pockets of his jeans.

Lucie swallowed. "Hi. You're...home."

"I...uh..." He shrugged. "Talked to Joey last night. Sounded like things were getting crazy so I took a few vacation days. You know I think Ro is a pain in the ass, but I love her."

And that fast, the jab in her chest morphed to something bigger. Something that formed a giant ball between her ribs and blocked her air. *Breathe.*

She couldn't. The last days, between Ro being arrested, Tim's irritation with her, and sneaking around behind his back to investigate, had drained her. And now—*damn it*—right in front of her stood Frankie. The one person who understood the insanity that came with being a mob boss's kid.

Lucie leaped from her chair and charged him. She wrapped her arms around his neck, squeezing so tight she might suffocate him.

"Ah, Luce," he said. "I'm so sorry."

She let out a hard breath, then inhaled the Frankie scent, the Tom Ford cologne she'd bought for him on every birthday and Christmas.

This year, she'd be buying for someone else.

"Luce? Are you okay?"

Standing on her tip-toes, she continued to hang on, resting her chin on his shoulder. She tried to speak, to say something, but the onslaught of emotions kept everything rooted inside so she did the only thing she could and managed to bob her head.

"Great," he said. "Nodding. That means you're not okay."

He knew her. Years together had forged a bond. One that allowed them to recognize each other's body language and mood swings. And hidden messages.

"I'm okay," she said. "I just...when I saw you, something inside me exploded."

"I know. Me too." He patted her back. "I thought I'd prepared myself for it."

"Frankie?"

"Yeah?"

"You smell nice."

"Thanks. Good to know."

She let out a laugh and backed away, holding on to his forearms.

"So," she said, "how are you? How's New York?"

"Are we really going to do this?"

"What?"

"Pretend like we're fine and can pick up as friends?"

Guess not. But he was right. She'd loved him too hard and for too long to think they could leave all that behind. Seeing him confused her and Tim didn't deserve that.

God, this sucked because she needed Ro right now. Ro would tell her the reaction to Frankie was normal and that she shouldn't become a headcase over it. Maybe she could call her?

Gee, Ro, I know you're locked up, but can you talk me off a ledge?

"Well," Lucie said, "I'm not sure friends is the right word. But our fathers are friends and you're Joey's best friend. We're going to see each other so we should be...nice."

"Nice." He shook his head. "Sounds peachy."

"I know. Somehow I never expected us to be analyzing our relationship boundaries."

He met her gaze again, held it for a long moment. Sad eyes. "Me neither, Luce."

"So," she said, "thanks again for coming. Joey needs the support right now and unfortunately, I've recently learned that I suck at keeping him under control."

"I heard you all were cellmates." He grinned. "That had to be cozy."

"Oh, ha, ha, smart guy."

Then Frankie stepped away, moving in a slow circle, taking in the room. They'd done a lot of decorating since he left, and Lucie felt a burst of pride at how much had been accomplished.

"I can't believe this is Carlucci's. My Dad said you guys did a great job, but—wow."

"It was all Ro. As crazy as she makes us, she has such an eye for style."

Frankie pointed to the pile of notes on her desk. "What's with the mess?"

"Just some notes. I ran out of paper and you know my mind, it never stops."

"Believe me, I know." He faced the rolling white board stowed against the wall and skimmed it. "You've been busy."

"I have. I can't let her sit in jail and do nothing. Not when I know she's innocent."

"You need help?"

Did she ever. Talking to Frankie seemed wrong, though. These last months Tim had been her first stop when she'd needed a sounding board. Tim was a good listener. The curious part of him was able to analyze situations and quickly form opinions. Which, she supposed made him a great detective. Now, with his limited knowledge of what she was doing with the Ro investigation, confiding in Frankie, in Lucie's mind, constituted a betrayal. No matter how alpha her hunky cop boyfriend was, that betrayal would hurt him and she wouldn't do that.

"I'd love another set of eyes on it, but I, um...need to talk to someone else about it first."

"O'Brien?"

Lucie wasn't sure how much Frankie had heard about her and Tim, but between Joey and everyone else in their hometown, he no doubt knew Lucie had a new boyfriend.

She nodded. "I think he'd be upset if I talked to you first."

"I know I'd be pissed."

"But after I talk to him, maybe you can look at all we've collected. You have that journalist's eye and might catch something."

"It's serious? With O'Brien?"

Yes.

She should say it. Right here, right now. Just put it out there. With the way she felt about Tim, the love she had for him, it should have been easy. And, yet, no. The words wouldn't come. She had loved Frankie too—part of her always would—and that left her emotions churning.

"Oh, Frankie. I really don't want to talk to you about this."

Again, he nodded. "I know. I just...I don't know. I guess we've been back and forth so many times that I thought," he met her gaze. "I thought we'd..."

"From a thousand miles away? How? Neither one of us is evolved enough for a commuter relationship."

"People do it, Luce."

"Not people like us."

Or maybe that had changed in the months since Frankie left. At least for him. Lucie? She still wanted her man close.

The doggie bells jangled and Lucie glanced over Frankie's shoulder. Tim entered and froze, his hand still on the open door, as cold air rushed in. He knew—all too well—of the Lucie/Frankie saga. It had, in fact, been a major issue for him when they'd first started dating. He'd told her, straight away, he wouldn't get involved with her if the relationship with Frankie still had a chance.

Tim wanted her free and clear.

And she adored that about him. The strength and level-headedness.

But this? Tim finding her and Frankie alone? Probably didn't look good.

She plastered on a smile even as the ball of panic unfurled inside her. "Hi."

The two men sized each other up. Not that she'd expect either of them to do any obnoxious posturing, but they were men after all.

She perked up, way too heavy on the cheery. "You remember Frankie."

Tim vacated the doorway, letting the door close behind him as he extended his hand. "I guess I should say welcome back. How's New York?"

"It's good." Frankie glanced at Lucie. "I miss the old neighborhood, but I love the job."

Tim wasn't stupid. He met Lucie's eye. "There's a lot to miss."

All righty then. Silence sucked all the energy from the room. Just gobbled it right up as the two men, opposites in many ways, yet truly the loves of Lucie's life, stared at her. Who knew she was such a man killer? Usually that fell into Ro's wheelhouse. *Well, move over, sister.* All Lucie needed now was her Wonder Woman gold cuffs.

A giggle bubbled up. That involuntary outburst that

plagued her during stressful situations. It was either that or flop peeing. Right now, she'd take the laugh.

Frankie smacked his hands together. "I don't want to keep you. I just got back and need to track Joey down."

Excellent idea. "He's probably walking Otis about now. He should be done soon though."

"I'll, uh, just meet him back at the house, I guess."

Frankie took a step toward her and she flinched, her eyes immediately going to Tim. "Okay," Frankie said, "I'll see you guys later, then."

Lucie nodded. Tim nodded. A couple of bobble heads they were. *Can we say awkward?* Tim waited for Frankie to leave and faced her. "You were laughing. What's funny?"

"Tim, I can honestly say, not one thing. I think I may have finally snapped. Over the edge. Run while you can."

"Is that what you want?"

What now? "I'm sorry?"

"For me to go. Is that what you want?"

"No!" She stepped closer and wrapped her arms around him. "Baby, no. It was a joke. A bad one I guess. All I ever want is you. You have to know that. I'm usually worried my life is too much for you. The chaos is never ending with the Rizzo bunch. And these last few days has only added to that."

"True that. I can take it though. Usually." He pulled free of her and gestured to the door. "Frankie being here. That surprised me."

"I didn't know. I promise you. He just walked in. He said Joey seemed upset, so he hopped on a plane this morning."

"Crap. He's a good guy."

Lucie smiled. "He is, but I'm kinda loving the good guy in front of me right now."

He looked down at her, met her gaze, and panic whipped up her spine.

"Tim, what is it?"

"Are you sure?"

"About?"

He glanced at the door. "Us, Luce. I see the way he looks at you. I look at you that way. I need you to be sure. I told you in the beginning I wouldn't do a back and forth thing with Frankie."

She slid her arms around him again, squeezing tight, and pressing her cheek into his chest. Her heart might be exploding and shattering at the same time. Big, tough, Tim O'Brien was afraid he'd lost her. On some level, it gave her a boost to know he loved her that much. On the other, more important level, he questioned her commitment to him.

And she couldn't have that.

"No way. I love you. You're the best man I know and you are always, always there for me. Besides, with a nickname like O'Hottie, I'd be a fool to let you go. And my mama didn't raise no fool."

His big hand came up and cradled the back of her head, holding her in place against him, all the heat from his body pouring into her. "I love you, Luce. Even if I'll be in a strait jacket by the time you're done with me."

He inched back and dipped his head, bringing his lips to hers and—*oh, yowza, yowza, yowza*—when Tim kissed her, it was like Christmas, her birthday and the fourth of July all rolled into one. One giant celebration of happiness and lust.

He brushed his lips against hers, doing that little sweeping motion he knew turned her on, then backed away, swatting her on the butt. "We'll finish this later. Now, tell me what's going on with this white board. Or don't I want to know?"

The white board. *Shoot.* She should have thrown a blanket over it or something.

"Don't freak," Lucie said.

"Ha!"

Funny man. "Listen, smart ass, they're just notes. I'm not investigating. Much."

Tim scratched at the back of his neck. She was probably giving him hives or some kind of stress-induced rash. And her without the Benadryl.

He let out a heavy breath. "You can't help yourself, can you?"

"Not when Ro is in jail. No."

"Alright then." He walked to the conference table and waggled a finger at her notes. "Tell me what you've got here."

Wait. What? He wanted to help? "Really?"

He turned back to her. "Yes. Really. That's why I'm here. I've been thinking about this mess. My boss won't let me help the PD. That leaves me one option. If you're not going to stop, the least I can do is make sure you don't cause havoc. I'll help you."

A burst of happiness exploded and Lucie threw her arms up, leaping at her man, who scooped her up. She wrapped her legs around him, whacking her ankle on the table. *Ow.* Who cared? She smacked a kiss on him, then did it again just for kicks. "Yay! Thank you."

Grinning like an idiot, he patted her rear. "You're welcome. And my back is glad you don't weigh a lot."

"Always a perk."

He eased her to the floor and she rushed back to her desk, scooped up the pile of notes, and deposited them on the conference table.

"Let's start with these." She picked up the brochure. "I

talked to a guy this morning. He delivers groceries to Buzzy and her neighbors."

She wouldn't say how she found him. No sense in getting the hot Irish detective all riled up. She shoved the brochure with the company name on it at Tim and he perused it, turning it sideways then upside down as he read her abbreviated notes.

"Where?"

"Where what?"

"Where did you talk to him?"

"It's not important."

"Oh, boy."

"What is important is that he told me Buzzy had a boyfriend."

"And?"

The dry-cleaning receipt came next and she handed it over. "He answered her door in his bathrobe once."

"You think he's a killer because he answered her door in his robe? You walk around my place in my T-shirts all the time. If I wind up dead, does that make you my killer?"

Lucie gasped. "Don't say that."

"Just making a point. You can't randomly accuse people of murder."

"I'm not randomly accusing him. It's a lead. That's all. She was killed inside her house. Obviously, her killer was inside so she must have let him in."

"A reasonable assumption." Tim gestured to the white board. "And what's this?"

"This is my murder board."

Really, she needed to lay off the crime shows.

"All right." He let out another long sigh. Poor guy. "Can you summarize?"

Gladly. She grabbed a marker and tapped it against the board. "Apparently, there was friction with Buzzy's agent."

"And you know this, how?"

"Buzzy's sister. And her assistant confirmed it. She told me Lorraine wanted Buzzy to dump the agent. Something about him doing funky accounting."

Now Tim grabbed a legal pad off the stack in the center of the table. Finally, she'd said something that caught the good detective's interest.

"I'll look into the agent."

"I have the Cock Heads on it as well."

"Oh, goodie." He finished his note and pointed to Dad's name on the board. "Do I even want to ask?"

"It's fine. Dad, Jimmy and Lemon are putting feelers out with their cop friends."

Tim grunted and Lucie threw up her hands. "Just to see if they have any information. That's all."

"You're destroying me. You know that, right? Every night I check my blood pressure."

Lucie rolled her eyes. "Stop. You know..." What? She shook her head. "I'm sorry I'm stressing you out. I love her. I'd do the same for you."

He grabbed her elbow, pulled her into him and kissed the top of her head. "I know. You worry me, Luce. This is a homicide. Someone killed this woman and you're running around asking questions. It could be dangerous."

"If it gets Ro out of jail it'll be worth it."

"I hope so."

13

———

Thump.

Something smacked against the shop window. Both Tim and Lucie jumped.

A growing group of pedestrians huddled on the side-walk in front of the shop.

Tim cocked his head. "Are those picket signs?"

One woman stood at the front of the pack, now extended beyond the shop's window, handing out poster boards attached to what looked like paint sticks. Talk about your grass roots protest. Lucie couldn't make out the writing yet, but as each person received their sign, they strolled the side-walk to the far end of the shop, turned, and headed back.

"What the heck?"

Tim let out a snort. "Why the hell do you have protestors?"

That question was quickly answered as the growing crowd sent up a chant.

"Mur-der-er! Mur-der-er! Mur-der-er!"

"For God's sake." Lucie's voice trembled and she fought to control the brewing hysteria.

Like annoying ants at a picnic, the protestors kept coming, each stepping up to receive a sign. *Please let them run out of signs.*

A young woman peered through the window, cupping her hands around her eyes. "Hey. She's in there."

The crowd let out a roar, all of them huddling up to the window. Their hateful, angry—well, that might have been an exaggeration—eyes zoomed in on Lucie.

Instinctively, she slid behind Tim, the big, hunky cop who carried a big, hunky gun.

"Murderers," an older woman screamed.

Lucie whipped her phone from her back pocket. By now Dad and the crew at Petey's would be saddling up. They didn't like strangers on their block.

"Who are you calling?"

"My dad. Can you see it? A bunch of mob guys versus angry protestors."

She lifted the phone to her ear. He picked up on the first ring. "Baby girl, don't you worry. Me and the boys are on it."

All she needed was a brawl in front of her place. "Dad, no. Please! Tell the guys they can't touch them. Someone will get arrested. You know how your friends get when they go off half-cocked."

"You worry too much." He hung up. Dear God.

"Luce," Tim wandered to the window. "Call the Franklin PD. Just let them know you have a hopefully peaceful protest going here."

Good thought. Joey had gone to high school with a guy who'd become a Franklin cop. Brian was a regular at Petey's and had an open rapport with Dad's crew. Maybe he could do something.

Not that she didn't believe in a citizen's right to protest.

She just didn't want them doing it in front of her shop with the fashion show caterer about to show up.

Chaos. Total chaos.

She was patched through to Brian, who had just gotten out of roll call.

"Brian. It's Lucie Rizzo."

"Hey, Lucie. I'm heading out. What's up?"

Another thunk sounded and she spun back, waving a fist at the window. "Off the window!"

"Yow," Brian said. "I need that ear, Lucie."

"Sorry. I think I need help. I have a bunch of protestors in front of my place."

"Why?"

"I'm not sure exactly. They keep saying 'mur-der-er, mur-der-er'."

"Oh-*kay*. Are they blocking the street?"

"No. They're on the sidewalk."

"Sorry, Lucie. There's nothing we can do. They have the right to be there."

Which Lucie knew. But really, did the Franklin PD want a bunch of protestors mixing it up with the Rizzo crime family? She met Tim's gaze and threw her free hand up.

"Brian?"

"Yeah?"

"Think about the location of my business and who my father is."

The line went silent and, for a second, Lucie wondered if she'd lost the connection. She checked the screen. Full bars.

"Crap," Brian finally said. "Is your Dad's crew there? Now?"

"Not yet, but he's sending them down. I don't want any trouble, and I know the guys like you. Maybe you can give everyone a speech or something. I don't know."

"I'll swing by."

Excellent. She punched off and her phone immediately rang.

Annabelle. The Cock Head. Maybe she had an update.

"Hi, Annabelle."

"I just saw on Buzzy's Facebook page about the protest. We're on our way."

"Who?"

"The Cock Heads, silly."

"You're *joining* the protest?"

Tim shot her a look, shaking his head the whole time.

"Of course not. What kind of friends would that make us? We're protesting their protest."

How awesome was that? True friends right there. "Oh, Annabelle. Thank you. I appreciate it, but you don't have to."

"You and Ro are good people. You don't deserve this. We're bringing it! They'll be sorry they messed with us."

Annabelle hung up. What was with everyone hanging up on her today? And what was this nonsense about a protest on Buzzy's Facebook page?

"The Cock Heads are forming a counter protest."

Tim laughed. "What?"

While he found amusement in Lucie's plight, she hopped over to Buzzy's page on her Facebook app and —*bam*—right there, pinned to the top was the announcement about the protest.

Lucie glanced outside at the growing crowd. These folks were early. This nightmare wasn't even scheduled to start for another—she checked the clock—fifty-two minutes. If she had this size crowd now, what would another hour bring?

"There's a post on Buzzy's Facebook page about it."

Tim peered over her shoulder. "Who the hell posted it?"

"I'm not positive, but I know from the fashion show meetings that Kandi—one of Buzzy's minions—does all the posting on that page. I can't imagine she organized a protest, though. I have a meeting with the caterer in a few minutes. After that, I'll call Kandi and ask about it. Right now I'm more worried about the counter protest the Cock Heads are mobilizing and, well, there's Jimmy Two-Toes, Slip and Lemon to contend with."

"Hang tight." Tim headed for the front door. "Let me see if I can do anything."

"Thank you. I love you."

"Love you too."

Lucie stowed her phone just as another protestor cupped his hands against the glass.

"Hey, hands off the glass."

Protesting was one thing, making a mess of her window was another. The man backed away then swung sideways, his mouth moving, his hands flapping.

Tim exited the shop, stopped, said something to the protestor then looked right. Jimmy Two-Toes marched up, his hands and mouth moving equally fast. The two men squared off with Tim between them.

So help her, if Tim got one scratch, she'd murder someone.

She hustled to the door, shoved it open.

"Get away from the building," Jimmy said to the man.

"It's a public street."

"You had your hands on the glass. And believe me, I know where you can have your hands and where you can't." He took a step closer. "Now back up."

Tim set his hand on Jimmy's shoulder. "Everyone settle down."

"Who are you to tell me—"

"Hey!" Lucie swung her finger at the two men. "Anyone gets violent, you're dead. Do you hear me?"

"Murderer," the man shouted. Another chant rose from the growing crowd.

Tim shot her a look. "Really?"

Yes. Really.

"Mur-der-er, mur-der-er, mur-der-er."

"Lucie," Jimmy said, "get inside. You can't be out here."

"Move it, people." At the far end of the sidewalk, Annabelle and the Cock Head brigade stormed toward them like paratroopers on a mission. Annabelle, of course, wore her signature Cock Head headband with the giant feathers poking skyward. "Let's go, Cock Heads. Line up."

"Here we go," Tim said.

Annabelle shoved by Jimmy, Tim and the protestor. "Make room. We're taking control of this sidewalk."

Jimmy screwed up his face. "Who the hell do you think you are?"

"We're the Cock Heads."

Oh, boy. The dozen or so Cock Heads formed a line in front of the store, their arms linked and blocking the entrance.

Protestor boy wasn't pleased. He also wasn't moving. "Hey," he said to the Cock Heads, "you can't block the sidewalk."

"Ha! Look who's talking? We're not blocking the sidewalk. We're keeping you lunatics from getting too close to this shop. It's private property. She can have you arrested."

"That's right," Jimmy said, suddenly fully onboard.

Holy crap. Dueling protests. Right in front of Coco Barknell. This was definitely not her marketing of choice.

Jimmy swung back and faced the line of Cock Heads. "Make room. Let me in."

Lord, she needed a picture of this. Jimmy Two-Toes lined up with the feather wearing Cock Heads and forming a human barrier to counter-protest the protest. Ro would not believe this one.

When Annabelle and Sam unlinked their arms for Jimmy to join them, Lucie scooted behind. One place she didn't want to be was the space between dueling protests.

Having heard enough, Tim flashed his badge. "Everyone stay calm and no one gets arrested. Understood?"

If anyone could control these nutcases it would be Tim.

"You can't touch us," Protest Boy said.

This guy, Lucie was sure, would be a nightmare. If she had to guess, he'd probably alerted the media by now.

Tim hung his badge on his belt and spread his hands wide. "Who said I'm touching you?"

"I'm just letting you know."

Tim laughed, turned away from Protest Boy, and faced Lucie. "You okay?"

"I'm fine."

"Cock Heads unite," someone yelled from the far end.

Probably Jamal. He was always good for some drama.

For added fun, Lemon and Slip headed down the sidewalk.

"Lemon," Jimmy said, "get in here. Link up so we can keep these pains in the asses from the shop. You take that end. Slip, down here. Nobody gets by. Nobody."

"You've got to be kidding me," Tim muttered.

Don't I wish. "It's insane. Can I get rid of them?"

"As long as they're peaceful, no. You're stuck with them."

Just then, a small white projectile—coming straight at Tim—caught Lucie's eye. She lifted her hand to block it, but...too late. An egg slammed into his shoulder, the shell shattering and yolk oozing on his spotless suit.

"Ah, damn it." He looked up at the roof and pointed. "Hey, dumbass. I'm a cop. Get down here, right now. What the hell is wrong with you?"

Lucie craned her head and spotted a young guy with dark hair, maybe mid-twenties, leaning over the brick, two more eggs in hand.

"Hey," she said, "you're trespassing. Get off my roof."

The kid blew raspberries at her. Seriously? Who does that?

Another egg flew. Straight at her. Tim lifted a hand and deflected it, winning another bout of oozing goo for his efforts.

"I gotta get this idiot down," he said. "Luce, get inside before he starts a riot."

A siren blared, letting off a quick *whup, whup* before going silent. "Franklin PD! All you protestors, get off the street. Right now."

Overhead the approaching *chuff, chuff, chuff* of a helicopter sounded. Lucie peered up. Channel seven news.

Yep. One of these protestors alerted the media. And why not? Between the murdered reality star and the mob boss's daughter, a reporter could exist on this high for a month. Total paradise.

"We've got press," Lucie said.

Tim pointed at the door. "Get inside while I deal with the egg thrower."

Brian, ablaze in his Franklin PD uniform, shoved through the crowd. "Lucie, is everything all right? I saw the guy on the roof toss something."

Tim badged Brian then pointed at the egg remnant on his shoulder. "Eggs."

Brian sighed. "There's always one."

"I'll head up there and grab him before he gets nuts. Can you handle the crowd down here?"

"Yeah. When I saw how big this thing was, I called for backup."

"Good." Tim grabbed Lucie's elbow, ushering her toward the door. "I'll climb the back fire escape. You need to stay inside. Preferably out of sight. It's peaceful right now, but all we need is one knucklehead."

"Like the one on the roof?"

"Exactly. One person can flip the switch on this thing. These people are protesting in front of your business, if you're out there, they might get more wired. Please stay inside."

Tim headed for the back door as Lucie watched the crowd outside. She hated standing in here, like a coward, when her friends were outside guarding her space. But Tim had a point. Her presence might prod an already motivated crowd into doing something that might get someone hurt.

As Lucie watched, Annabelle broke off from the human chain and popped through the front door. Lucie wrapped her arms around her. "Annabelle, thank you for this. You guys didn't have to come here."

"I knew it would be a lot. People are crazy, Lucie."

This from a woman with peacock feathers protruding from her head.

"That they are."

"I was going to call you today anyway." Annabelle swiveled back to check the door, then leaned in close. "I have information."

Unless they had bionic hearing, no one could hear her. "Um, Annabelle? We're alone in here."

And my brother has dispatched with all the bugs.

"Oh, good. I hate whispering. It feels so dirty. Anyway, we did the research on Buzzy's agent. It's not good news."

"Really? Do tell."

"Well, I dug around on the internet and found some obscure articles from six months ago. Not about Buzzy, but the agent. One of his other clients fired him. Something about a difference of opinion on financial matters."

"Lucky for us, financial matters are my wheelhouse."

Annabelle dug around in her handbag and pulled out some folded papers. "I know! I printed you copies of the articles. It might not matter though."

"Why?"

"Because Buzzy, from what I could tell, hadn't fired him. He was still her agent of record. And, well, he was in L.A. at a movie premiere the night of the murder."

Talk about burying the lead. If the agent was in L.A., he couldn't have been in Buzzy's house, killing her with an atomic wedgie. "Shoot. Really? You're sure?"

Annabelle handed over another printout. "Pictures. This is him in front of the step-and-repeat. You know, we should get one of those for the Cock Heads. How fun would that be?"

Ro was rotting in jail, the most promising lead just evaporated, and Annabelle was pondering a step and repeat.

Lucie studied the photo in front of her. *Darn it.* She'd been so sure the agent might be involved. A setback, for sure, but these things happened during investigations. Disappointment wouldn't derail her. No way. Ro was innocent and she'd prove it.

"Okay, Annabelle. Thanks so much."

"I know it's not what you wanted to hear."

"That's true, but you've saved me a lot of research time. I'm so appreciative. And Ro too."

"What else can we do?"

Outside, a load roar came from the crowd. Lucie looked up to see Protest Boy standing on the hood of someone's car. If it belonged to one of the guys from Petey's, they'd have bloodshed. Lucie squeezed Annabelle's arm. "I'm not sure. I'll let you know if I think of something though."

Protest Boy was hauled off the car by someone, Brian most likely, just as Tim came through the back door, shoving the egg thrower in front of him.

"You," she said, "you just ruined my boyfriend's suit."

The kid ripped off a smug grin and Lucie curled her fingers into a tight fist. Violence had never been her thing, but lately, jerky people had pushed her buttons.

"Wipe that smile off your face. You're paying for that suit. So help me, if it's the last thing I do, you're paying for it."

"Good luck," the kid said.

Oh, a tough guy. Perfect. "I don't need luck. Ask me my name."

The kid held his hands up and waggled his fingers. "Ooh, now I'm scared. But I'll bite. What's your name?"

"Seriously?" Tim said, "Dude, you're on her roof throwing eggs and you don't even know who she is?"

This would be fun. For the first time, she understood why Joey always asked people who messed with him if they knew his name. Lucie? For years she'd been running from it, from the fear her father's name instilled. At least until today. "My name," she said, "is Lucie. Lucie *Rizzo*."

A little of the smug came off the kid's face, so Lucie took a step closer. "Yes, *that* Rizzo. Let it sink in. After it does, you're going to apologize to this handsome man for ruining a perfectly good suit."

The kid swung his head to Tim. "I'm sorry. Sorry. I'll pay

you for it. I swear to God, I'll pay you for it." He came back to Lucie. "I didn't know."

As if it was acceptable to throw eggs at people who didn't happen to be the boyfriend of a mob boss's daughter? Well, Lucie had had enough. She grabbed a pen and paper. "I don't care. What you did was wrong. Let me see your ID. I want your name and address and we'll contact you with the cost of the suit. And you'd better pay it. "

"I will. I promise."

"Next time think about what you're doing. There are consequences to everything."

Like sending a stupid tweet. A stupid tweet that landed Ro in jail.

Protest or no protest, business had to be done. With Ro out of pocket and the picketers apparently not going anywhere, Lucie needed a place—chaos free—to conduct her meeting.

Short on options other than the local library, she left Coco Barknell in the capable hands of the Franklin PD and moved her meeting to her former company headquarters.

Otherwise known as Mom's dining room.

At least there they'd have quiet. And, more than likely, cake. Sometimes, Mom's cake made bad days a whole lot brighter. Something she needed.

On the upside, by the time she'd left the shop, Officer Brian had convinced Dad's crew to head back to Petey's before the feds showed up in search of some obscure charge to slap on them. Plus, with Dad being on parole, Lucie couldn't risk him being locked up again. Mom had just adjusted—somewhat anyway—to him being home and

Lucie wouldn't be responsible for sending him back to the slammer.

Sigh.

She arrived at Mom's, unpacked her laptop and notepad, and—*voila*— the doorbell rang. Mom had finally convinced Dad to ditch the theme from the Godfather as a bell chime, but the compromise came by way of the famous Italian song "Quando, Quando, Quando."

Lucie swung the front door open and greeted Reece. She wore her black coat over a slim skirt and loose blouse with red crystal earrings. Her blond hair hung over her shoulders and she gave it a swipe as she walked.

"Hi." She walked past Lucie, averting her eyes.

"Hi," Lucie said.

Reece held up a folder. "Carmen got hung up in another meeting. She sent me the menu choices for us to review."

Whatever. "That's fine. We'll look at it in the dining room." But first, they needed to deal with the protest elephant in the room. "Before we do that, we need to talk about the picketers."

Reece dipped her chin. "I'm so sorry about that."

Oh, wasn't this rich. She was sorry? Sorry! "Forgive me, Reece, but you can't be that sorry, since you didn't bother to give me a heads up. Knowing how rabid Buzzy's fans are and that we still have a fashion show to put on together, why would Foo-Foo organize a protest of my business? Via Facebook!"

"It wasn't my idea."

"Who posted that message about the protest? Was it Kandi?"

"I can't say."

Fine. Another one who thought she could push around Joe Rizzo's kid. Lucie rose from the table. "Then we'll head back to my shop, where a horde of reporters begged me for a statement as I was leaving. But in the spirit of partnership—something certainly not shown to Coco Barknell—I decided not to comment until I spoke to someone at Foo-Foo. You're not willing to help me, so I'll just round up a couple of reporters and drop well-placed tidbits about Buzzy stealing our designs." Lucie snapped her fingers. "And, oh, right, you trying to discredit us with a damned protest. With all the media attention surrounding Buzzy's death, I'm sure the press will eat that drama right up. I mean, *Buzzy* a fraud? An intellectual property thief? Who'd have guessed that?"

On a roll now, all that stirred up anger soaring, she whipped around, heading for the door.

"Lucie! Wait."

Ah. Better.

Lucie paused. "You need to help me understand."

Reece screwed her face into pinched misery.

She thought she was upset? *Puh-lease.* "Start talking, Reece."

"Don't go to the press. I'm begging you. Things are insane at the office. *Lorraine* is insane. Every time she walks into the building the entire staff tries to hide. It's like an episode of *Survivor.*"

Now they were blaming Lorraine? "Her sister died. She's grieving. Maybe you guys could give her some slack."

"Yes, but we're running a business and Lorraine is walking around barking orders at us. Nobody knows what to do. The executives try to keep her out of the building, but she's Buzzy's sister. How do they kick her out?"

A tough one indeed. "I stopped at the house the other day. She must be under a tremendous amount of stress."

"Sure, but you're being generous making excuses for her.

She was the one who told Kandi to schedule that damned protest."

"*Lorraine* wanted it? Why?"

"I have no idea. She came in yesterday all kinds of crazy. She parked in Buzzy's office and started boxing things up. When I asked if I could help, she went off about Roseanne killing Buzzy and how angry she was. She told me to get a protest going. I think she wants you and Roseanne to feel bad. You know, guilty, about Buzzy."

"We do feel bad. Nobody deserves that, but Ro is innocent."

"Lorraine doesn't think so. And since they arrested Ro..." Reece shrugged.

"As if no other people in Buzzy's life were mad at her? What about her boyfriend?"

"Which one?"

Whoopsie. Apparently Buzzy—God rest her soul—was doing the nasty with multiples. "She had more than one?"

Again, Reece shrugged. "She liked men. Dated a lot. I don't know the details though. You'd have to ask Lorraine."

Terrific. More suspects to hunt down, but somehow Lucie didn't think Reece would pony up any names. Then again, if there were multiple men in Buzzy's life...

Ask Lorraine.

There's an idea. Lorraine had been civil to Lucie when she'd been at the house. She could use her confusion over the protest as an excuse for a meeting and while there, if she got lucky, she'd pump Lorraine for information about Buzzy's boyfriends.

Lucie had a lead to follow.

Nothing said tragedy like a pack of jealous lovers.

Using her successful dog walking/snooping excursion the day before as a barometer, Lucie scored a parking space two blocks over from Buzzy's still-barricaded street. Intending to cut through the yard of the vacant house, she walked one block and turned, but was interrupted by her ringing phone.

For the love of Pete. Lucie couldn't leave the office for a little reconnoitering without people hunting her down. All this Ro being in jail nonsense was a major PITA.

Maybe she'd take a stand, for once be irresponsible, and not answer the phone. She considered that option, but with the protest still in play, probably not a wise choice.

She checked her phone. 312 number. Could be anyone. Might as well answer it. "This is Lucie."

A short pause ensued and just as she was about to hang up a recording announced a collect call from an inmate at the Cook County jail.

Ro.

Holy cannoli. The recording droned on and Lucie bobbed her head. "Come on, come on, put her through already."

Finally, the magic question was asked. Would she accept the call?

"Yes," Lucie said. The line clicked. Silence. "Ro? Are you there?"

"Oh, my God," her BFF said, her voice rising to just shy of drama queen. "I could have taken a nap while they connected this damned call. I should lodge a complaint about my phone time being wasted on subpar service."

Even locked up, Ro did a great holier-than-thou act. "Are you okay? What's going on?"

"Nothing. I just...missed you. And Joey got an account set up so I could call cell phones or land lines. He's really good at this, you know."

Her brother. The corrections expert.

"He's had practice with my dad. But I don't want to talk about them right now. Gosh, I'm so happy to hear your voice."

"I know. It's crazy how much I take for granted." Ro let out a little sigh. "Never again, Luce. When I get out of here, I will appreciate every taste of freedom."

A car stormed down the block with the precision of an Indy racer, the driver managing not to hit the parked bumper to bumper vehicles.

Relieved at the normalcy—well, kinda—of chatting with Ro, Lucie leaned against a tree in front of the vacant house.

"I only have a few minutes," Ro said. "There's a line for the phone. And these bitches get mean."

Oy. Lucie didn't want to think about prisoner improvised weapons. Chair leg nunchuks, toilet paper shivs, spears made from bedposts. All of it scared the daylights out of her. Bad enough Dad liked to share those war stories over dinner conversation.

"I'm so sorry," Lucie said. "I promise, we're working on getting you out. I'm at Lorraine's now. Apparently Buzzy had a few boyfriends. I'm looking into that. And the agent? He's a bust. He was at a movie premiere the night of the murder."

"He could have hired someone."

"Could have. If this boyfriend thing doesn't pan out, we'll look into that." So what if the call was being recorded? If the cops weren't already on the agent, they would be now. "Have you talked to Willie? Where are they on the security video from Buzzy's house? Last I heard, detectives were trying to get their hands on the security company's records."

"Eh," Ro said. "No movement. The cops got a warrant, but the company is in no rush to release the backups. Willie said it's not unusual since this is after the fact."

Lucie let out a growl. "So, if a life were in danger, they'd release them. But since she's already kicked they won't? Lovely. I'll talk to—"

Tim.

Can't say that when being recorded.

"Luce? You there?"

"I'm here. I'll get into it and let you know what I find."

"Thank you."

The sound of clicking heels drew Lucie's gaze to an extremely pulled-together brunette in a long white coat marching up the walkway of the vacant house. This woman screamed success. And confidence. Who had the spine to wear a white coat in Chicago in the dead of winter? One splash through dirty snow and that coat was toast.

The brunette paused at the oversized—and crooked—realtor sign shoved into the frozen patch of lawn. She gave it a useless push and shook her head. Lucie studied the photo on the sign, then shifted back to the woman.

Realtor.

"Luce?"

"I'm here. Keep your head up in there. Okay? We'll get you out, I swear to you."

"I'm okay. I'm in the good wing. And, hey, I'm brushing up on my gin rummy. There's a nightly card game. Cocktails at seven. Black tie required."

Good old, Ro. Always finding the humor.

"As soon as we get you out, I'll play you. I'm pretty good at gin rummy, you know."

"Deal."

On Ro's end of the line, someone hollered something about losing daylight. "Oh, go slap yourself," Ro shot back.

Cripes, maybe she shouldn't be aggravating felons.

Watch out for the toilet paper shivs.

"Luce, I have to go before these girls string me up."
"Don't say that!"
"I love you, Luce."
"Love you too. And don't worry. We'll get you out."
If it kills me, we'll get you out.

14
———

Lucie disconnected Ro's call just as the realtor popped the lock box open on the brownstone. She glanced up and... *Whoa, wait one second.*

The day before, Lucie had been too preoccupied with sneaking onto Buzzy's street to notice the security camera above the door of the vacant home. Did the back entrance also have one?

The realtor made quick work of unlocking the door as Lucie strode to the end of the walkway.

"Excuse me," she called.

The woman swung back and offered up a welcoming smile. "Yes? Can I help you?"

You sure can. "I'm Lucie Rizzo. I'm a...private investigator."

A snort-worthy declaration, no doubt, but not a total lie. This *was* an investigation and she *was* a private person.

"An investigator?"

The woman's face fell. Just plop. Maybe that private investigator line wasn't such a good one.

"Yes. I'm looking into the murder that occurred on the next block."

"Oh, that's just horrible. I'm so relieved they caught the person. In this neighborhood, a crime like that? It's murder on comps." The woman shuddered.

"Yes, well," Lucie said. "I see this home has a security camera above the door. I'm sure the police have inquired about it, but since you're here, I thought I'd ask."

"I see." The realtor inched backward over the threshold with an *I-swear-I-don't-know-anything* look plastered on her face.

Time to get a little aggressive. Not wanting to spook the woman, Lucie remained in her spot. "I hate to bother you, but it's imperative that all information be given to the police."

"Why? They arrested someone."

"The case is circumstantial. At best."

That halted the realtor's retreat. "What? They might have the wrong person?"

Not might. "It's a possibility. Imagine what *that* revelation would do to home values."

For a second, the woman stared at Lucie, her face a mix of confusion and doubt. Time to pull out the big guns.

"I apologize for bothering you, but this really is a matter of public safety. If we could get a copy of the video, it might show suspicious activity around the house."

"I'm not authorized to release any videos. I can contact the owners though and ask them to call you."

Dang it. Minor setback. Lucie hadn't come this far to walk away empty handed. Time for plan B.

If only she had a plan B.

"I'm sorry," the realtor said, "I have an appointment."

"I understand. I'll let you go, but..." Total longshot here.

"Is there any chance you could show me the video from the night of the murder?"

She wasn't Joe Rizzo's kid for nothing.

Now the woman stepped fully inside, wrapped her hand around the door, and started closing it. "I'm sorry. I can't help you. I'll call the owner though. Call my office." She poked a finger at the sign. "If the owner says it's okay to give you his number, I'll do that. Sorry."

And, she's gone.

Total bust. Two good possibilities, first the agent and now the newfound security system, had netted her a big whopping zilch. Every tiny lead seemed to be blowing up. She fought the absolute crush of frustration in her shoulders. Something had to give or Ro would be facing a jury.

Tim.

She'd fire off a text and let him know the house behind Buzzy's had video security. *Damn it.* What they really needed was Buzzy's backup video from the security company. How a corporation could sit on a warrant involving a murder, Lucie couldn't bend her mind around.

Heck, maybe she'd call them too. Hit them with her private detective line and see what happened. Nothing to lose.

The neighbor's security might be a stretch, but if Lucie could get a look at Buzzy's? She might be able to wrap this whole thing up.

She pounded out the text, added a couple of hearts and an *I love you,* and tapped the send button. He wouldn't be happy with her butting in again, but...oh well. These last couple of months the hot, Irish detective had been toughening up, getting used to Lucie and the insanity known as her life.

Anticipating his response, she powered the phone down.

Why allow herself to be distracted with an unhappy boyfriend?

Denial. Sometimes a girl's best friend.

She tucked the phone in her purse and made her way down the alley, cutting across Buzzy's backyard to the rear of Lorraine's house. If she did this quickly, she'd be at Lorraine's front door before the cops at either end of the block spotted her.

"Wonder Womaannnn," she sang in a quiet voice as she sneaked through Lorraine's gate.

Coming here unannounced had been a risk. Hopefully one that would come out in Lucie's favor. The element of surprise and all that. If she'd called, Lorraine might have put her off. Particularly with the whole protest fiasco. Now, showing up at the door—assuming her target was even at home—made it harder for Lorraine to send her away.

"Wonder Womaannnn."

She poked the bell.

A lyrical chime sounded followed by a squawk. Either Lorraine had taken custody of Felix, or she had her own crazy parrot.

The door opened and Lucie pasted on a sort-of smile. Nothing too over the top.

The little crease between Lorraine's eyebrows deepened and her head snapped back. "Lucie. Hello."

Ah, yes. The element of surprise. "Hi."

Struck mute, Lorraine simply stared.

"Um," Lucie said, "can I come in for a second?"

Lorraine bopped herself on the forehead and stepped back, holding the door open. "Of course. I'm so sorry. My brain is...gone. Did we have an appointment scheduled?"

"No. I took a chance coming by."

"I see."

"I hope that's okay."

"Not a problem at all. I'd planned to call you today anyway."

Huh. What was this now? "About?"

Lorraine led Lucie into the large kitchen where white stone countertops gleamed and French doors anchored a wall of windows. The tiny yard backed up to the row of homes on the next block.

The kitchen, although the same shape as Buzzy's, was more modern with smooth gray cabinets, slick handles, and stainless appliances. Buzzy's kitchen? Traditional. Dark woods and warm paint all the way. How different the sisters' tastes were.

In the sea of cool tones, sat a burst of hot pink. Buzzy's tablet. Lucie recognized the giant *BS* on the cover. Early on, Lucie and Buzzy had shared a laugh over how it could, depending on Buzzy's mood, represent her initials or the bullshit she dealt with on any given day.

"Don't fucking do it! 5511! Piss off!" Felix squawked, the sharpness carrying from the adjoining room.

Here we go again.

Lorraine rubbed her palm up her forehead. "That bird. He never stops."

The strain in her voice, the defeat that came with devastating loss, brought Lucie's gaze back to Lorraine's puffy eyes. The woman had to be beat.

Losing her sibling would be enough to derail Lucie, never mind living next door to the crime scene and having to deal with Buzzy's affairs. In fact, when Lucie left here, she'd hunt down her idiot, lug of a brother and hug him. Just because she could.

"Don't fucking do it! 5511! Piss off!"

Lorraine grunted. "He does this all day and night. Just

keeps screaming. Why couldn't my sister have taught him nice words?"

"I wonder if he's mourning. I know dogs go through grief when they lose someone. I suppose a parrot could."

"I don't know. He's driving me crazy though. There is no sleep to be had around here."

"I'm so sorry, Lorraine."

She motioned Lucie to a stool at the breakfast bar. "Thank you. But this isn't fair to you. Since you're here and I was going to call you anyway, let's talk business. I looked into the issue with the designs."

Ro's designs.

Lorraine sat on the stool beside Lucie and swiveled to face her. Good. With the amount of money at stake, Lucie preferred looking straight at her, searching for any sign of deception. "And?"

"The lawyer would kill me for saying this, but I don't know what my sister was thinking selling those designs without some sort of agreement in place."

Translation: Buzzy stole them, but Lorraine wouldn't admit it. What they had here was a negotiation. One that would compensate Coco Barknell, but save face for Buzzy.

Still, a sense of relief washed over Lucie. At least now, maybe they could avoid a court battle that would cost everyone a bundle.

"Don't fucking do it! 5511! Piss off!"

That bird. Crazy. Lucie's eye went to Buzzy's tablet and the BS on the cover. She knew what the BS stood for today. "What do you propose?"

"Normally, when my sister does distribution deals, the partner gets 10%."

Ten percent! Ridiculous. Lucie opened her mouth, but Lorraine held up a hand. "*Normally* most folks are thrilled with that. The percentage is small, but my sister's name creates volume. In the first week, most entrepreneurs make more than they would in twenty years of selling the product on a smaller scale."

The logic was sound, but this wasn't about money. Not completely. These were Ro's designs. She deserved the credit.

"Lorraine, ten percent won't do it. I'm sorry."

"I know. Which is why, as a goodwill gesture to make this go away and let me get on with dealing with my sister's estate, I'm going to offer you fifty percent. Plus, your company will get credit for the design."

Fifty percent. Plus a credit. Lucie did some quick math and...holy cow. That Fortune 500 dream might not be out of the question.

But she'd play this cool. Not let her excitement take over. First things first. She needed to speak to Ro. These were her designs. This decision, they'd make together.

"Thank you, Lorraine. I appreciate you seeing our side of this. Obviously, I need to speak to my team. Can I get back to you in a day or two?"

"Don't fucking do it! 5511! Piss off!"

"Of course. And, I just realized, you came here to talk to me and I didn't even give you a chance. What can I help you with?"

Somehow, after receiving her offer, demanding the woman not organize protests against Coco Barknell seemed rude. And requesting the names of her sister's boyfriends even more so.

How the heck could she even transition to that?

The cordless rang—*phew*—and Lorraine glanced down at it. "Lucie, I'm so sorry. I have to take this. It will only take five minutes. Do you mind? Then, I promise, you'll have my undivided attention."

Saved by the bell. Literally. "Sure," Lucie said. "Take your time."

Lorraine scooped up the phone and left the kitchen, obviously heading somewhere for privacy.

The few extra minutes gave Lucie time to pull a topic out of her rear. Something about the fashion show. The menu. Beef or chicken?

Ugh. She needed better than that.

"Don't fucking do it! 5511! Piss off!"

The flash of hot pink still on the counter drew Lucie's eye. In one of her early meetings with Buzzy, they'd discussed a file that Buzzy needed. The file however, was on her laptop and she hadn't had it with her. The tablet proved handy when she logged into her online backup system and retrieved the file.

Lucie cocked her head. Did the security system backup to the online system? If she could get on the tablet...

"Don't fucking do it! 5511! Piss off!"

If Felix hadn't been screaming that same series of phrases since the other night, Lucie would consider it a warning.

Now? With all of her leads fizzling out, not so much.

She swiveled on the stool and checked the hallway. No Lorraine.

Hmmm... Total invasion of privacy.

Ro in jail.

Yeah, much worse.

Decision made, she slid the tablet over, flipped open the cover and tapped the button. The password screen lit up.

Four digits.

"Don't fucking do it! 5511! Piss off!"

"Crazy bird."

Wait. 5-5-1-1. Four digits. Lucie opened her mouth. Shut it again. Could it be? She checked the hallway again—no Lorraine—and took a shot. Why not? That nutty bird kept hollering the number. Maybe it meant something.

She poked at the keypad. 5-5-1-1.

A small click sounded and—*bingo*—the Foo-Foo Entertainment logo popped up on the screen.

I'm in.

A surge of energy zinged straight up her arms. In the words of the immortal Joey: *Holy shit. This is it.*

The first solid break to freeing Ro.

Buzzy's favorite locations filled the screen and Lucie tapped the backup site. Could she get this lucky? If Buzzy kept the password stored on the tablet, yes, she could.

The login appeared, the fields automatically populating, and Lucie's heart started to pound.

She shouldn't do this. It had to be trespassing. At the very least, unauthorized access.

Worth the jail time?

Absolutely.

She peeped back over her shoulder. Still no Lorraine.

Trespassing or not, this was her chance. An opportunity to see if a video backup from the night of the murder existed. If she thought too long and hard about it, she'd get caught. Five minutes Lorraine had said.

Five minutes.

Running on adrenaline, Lucie logged in and went straight for the left sidebar. Two clicks later, a list of dates appeared. She clicked on the date of the murder and—*whoa* —Buzzy had a lot of files. Documents, spreadsheets, photos. What she needed was an mp4. Easy. She sorted by file type and found the video files.

Yes! All the backups were there. Months' worth. Lucie nearly cried. Now, she had evidence and everyone would see Ro was innocent. She scanned the dates on the folders, each in chronological order. One folder per day.

Easy. Peasy.

The magic date was December 6. Once Lucie had that, assuming the backup was the original, Ro would be proven innocent.

Free as a bird.

Lucie scrolled down the list, pausing at the end of November, slowly reading each date. Weird tension consumed her, kept her glued to the chair. Her fingers trembled with excess energy.

December 6. That's all she needed.

She continued reading. December 1, 2, 3...

"Don't fucking do it! 5511! Piss off!"

Lucie flinched. *Psycho bird.* She could see where he'd get annoying. She glanced down the hall. Still no Lorraine, but those five minutes were easily over. *Get moving, sister.* Lucie refocused on the list of dates.

December 4, 5, 7.

Wait. What the heck?

She had to have missed it. She scanned the list again, slowing at December 1 and reading each date. No December 6.

Just stop it.

The sense of anticipation vanished like a tornado out of steam. Lucie sagged forward, her eyes still on the screen.

Where the hell is it?

"Don't fucking do it! 5511! Piss off!"

She wouldn't panic. No sir. These online programs got hinky sometimes. Could be a fluke. She tapped the date field at the top of the screen and the video sort changed from newest to oldest. She tapped it again and resorted.

No December 6.

The file was gone.

Gone.

Gone.

Gone.

"Lucie?" Lorraine's voice sounded from behind her, "what are you doing?"

AFTER STRIKING OUT ON FINDING AN AWOL SUSPECT, TIM walked into the bullpen at headquarters and immediately sensed...something. The stench of burned coffee lingered. Someone must have left the burner on with only a swig left in the pot. One day these dumbasses would torch the place.

Three other detectives sat at their crappy desks—in equally crappy chairs—covered with notepads, files, and random bits of personal items. All of them glanced up, muttered a hello of some sort, and went back to whatever held their attention.

Having worked with the guys in his squad for a few years, Tim understood their moods. Tension was a potent thing. No matter what the situation, a breaking case, a fresh situation, a devastating day of testimony, whatever, it left a silent rumble in the air. An undercurrent that streamed and vibrated.

Or the tension could have been his own dread over facing his lieutenant with an update that equaled zilch.

After dealing with that crazy protest, an eyewitness suddenly having amnesia, and—oh, right—Frank Falcone showing up, his day was firmly in the crapper.

He got to his desk, dumped his phone and keys, and slid off his suit coat. A few texts had come in, but he had a call to make regarding said amnesiac witness before he got caught up in any distractions.

Darnell Banks hung up his phone and glanced over at him. "You pissy? You look pissy and we don't need that around here."

Excellent. Confirmation that the tension wasn't his imagination. "What's up?"

Darnell jerked his head sideways. "Lou is behind closed doors. Conference call with the brass."

"Why?"

"Don't know. Sneider murder. Maybe."

Tim dropped into his chair sending the springs into a squeaking fit. "Something pop?"

He never took to calling on the Lord to help solve a case, but he was sure an ulcer was starting over Ro being incarcerated. Lucie's general involvement in the whole mess ripped his guts out.

So, yeah, today, he'd ask the good Lord for some assistance on finding this killer.

Darnell lifted a hand. "All I know is the call came in. Lou told everyone not to bug him and that was that."

"Then I guess we wait."

Tim tapped his phone to scroll his texts. One from Lucie. Telling him she was going to Lorraine's. Tim slid the top drawer open and reached for his travel tube of antacids. He popped two, added a third for insurance, and finished reading the text that informed him the house behind Buzzy's had video monitoring.

His girl, in an obvious end run because she knew she was ripping his guts out, followed it up with two heart emojis and an I love you. No one would ever accuse her of being stupid.

He sat back and sighed.

"You okay?" Darnell wanted to know.

"Yeah. It's been one hell of a long week today."

He tapped Lucie's name and waited for the call to connect. Straight to voicemail. The little witch had turned her phone off.

God, he loved her.

He scratched an itch on the side of his face. The one that had sparked the second he saw Frankie in Lucie's shop. He'd been anticipating Mr. Slick's return, but had hoped he'd have a warning. A day at least to mentally prepare for Lucie seeing her first love again.

Tim knew Lucie loved him. Didn't doubt it for a second.

The problem was, she'd loved Frankie too. And sometimes that messed with one's mind. He couldn't get twisted about it. Couldn't. He'd told her from the beginning he wasn't interested in a love triangle. He wanted her and only her. Caveman that he was, he expected the same.

Period.

His lieutenant's door opened and Lou stuck his head out. "O'Brien, get in here. We have a development."

15

———

A development.

Just what he needed.

Tim strode into his boss's cramped office, taking the metal-framed chair Lou pointed to. Budgets being what they were, the city didn't splurge on furniture. Hell, most of the time they were grateful for whatever they got.

He settled into the chair, resting his hands on his thighs, and met his boss's dark gaze. "Problem?"

What this could be, he wouldn't even attempt a guess. Between his cases and Lucie, anything was possible.

"No. The Sneider case." Lou circled a hand. "I know you have a personal connection here."

Tim's stomach clenched. Up to now, he had been boxed out of any case details. Why did his boss suddenly want to discuss it with him? Unless one of the homicide guys had squealed that Tim inquired about Buzzy's agent. Hell, he hadn't even had a chance to tell Lucie they'd cleared the guy and Tim was already in a jackpot over it.

"I just got off a call," Lou said. "The backup of the security video was deleted from the victim's account. The company is checking to see if they might be able to pull it from their system. Backup of a backup type thing."

Tim's heart began a steady thump and he let out an easy breath. Maybe this wasn't about the agent.

The lack of a backup wasn't great news, but it might not be a total loss. Even with the backup being deleted from Buzzy's end, recovering it from the security company's system might be a possibility.

"Who deleted it?"

"We're looking into that. Whoever it was, logged in as Buzzy Sneider."

"After the fact."

Lou jerked his head.

Which meant someone who had Buzzy's login blew that file away. Call him cynical, but Tim didn't know a whole lot of people who gave out the logins to their home security system. Even with her army of assistants, would the woman actually give out her password?

"Had to be someone close to her."

Again, Lou jerked his head. "The homicide guys wanted me to ask, given your *relationship* with Lucie Rizzo, if you have ideas on who that person might be. Perhaps Lucie said something."

For months, Tim had anticipated the brass asking questions about Lucie and her family. He'd always assumed he'd be outraged over the PD using him to build a case. The case being against Roseanne, and not Joe Rizzo, boggled the mind.

Now that the question had finally come?

No outrage.

Not even a little. He sat back, pondered his conversations with Lucie. The theft of the designs, the pending lawsuit, the meetings with Buzzy's sister.

Lorraine.

Who Lucie had just texted him about. A wildcard, that one. Before Buzzy's death, Tim hadn't heard much, if anything about her.

But...

"Crap," he said.

"What?"

Tim pushed out of the chair, already moving to the door. "The sister. See what they know about her."

LUCIE WHIRLED AROUND. LORRAINE STOOD IN THE DOORWAY, her gaze shooting to the tablet. *Caught.*

Improvise. That's what she'd do. A little soft shoe to save her own butt. All those years of watching her father's legal battles had taught her a thing or twenty.

"Hi." She pointed at the tablet. "It was, um, making a noise. Beeping."

Beeping? *Lame, lame, lame.*

Lorraine's fierce look indicated exactly what she thought of Lucie's so-called beeping noise. She strode toward her, her steps swift and precise, and Lucie took a tiny step back. Lorraine scooped up the tablet, studied the screen, and a vein in her temple bulged. A big, nasty bulge. Lucie inched back another step.

"You're snooping in my sister's files? How did you even get in?"

"Don't fucking do it! 5511! Piss off!"

Well, that answered that question.

Lorraine stomped toward the connecting archway leading to the study, her bare feet smacking against the tile.

She poked her finger in Felix's direction. "You asshole bird. Shut up! I hate you."

Alrighty then. Felix wasn't exactly getting the love from Auntie Lorraine.

Time to go.

Lucie held up both hands. "This seems to be a bad time. I'll come back later. And...I'm sorry I snooped in Buzzy's files. My intentions were good. Truly. I'd heard Buzzy had been dating someone. That's why I came here. To ask you about the man. See if he might be a suspect. When you left the room, I thought I'd see if I could find the backup of the security video. That's all. Believe me, I want to find your sister's murderer as much as you do."

"The police have *arrested* Roseanne." She punched the tablet in the air. "The security video doesn't matter."

"It's not there anyway."

Lucie knew that already. It sat like a block of cement in her stomach. She'd failed Ro. Her BFF, her soul sister. From the time they were kids, Ro had been her protector. Even when they disagreed, Ro had been steadfast in her support. The bury-the-body person, they'd often joked.

Now they literally had a body and Lucie was helpless. Road blocks everywhere.

Miserable over her failure, she shook her head. "I'm sorry, Lorraine, I've overstepped here."

"You certainly have. Now get out."

Gladly. She scooped up her handbag remembering she needed to turn her phone back on when she got to the door. As soon as she left, she'd call Tim, let him know that she was done investigating. That he was right. She didn't belong in the middle of a police matter. All this running around, accomplishing nothing, and ignoring her work wouldn't help either. If the company failed, Ro wouldn't have a job to come home to.

If she came home.

Damn it.

Lucie slid her purse onto her shoulder then turned back to Lorraine, still holding that tablet.

The backup. Gone.

"Don't fucking do it! 5511! Piss off!"

Poor Felix. That little guy might be suffering from trauma over seeing his owner murdered. If only he could tell them what he saw.

Lucie halted as a wicked hiss stung her ears.

December 6. The day of the murder. No video. The only day missing. Last Lucie checked, dead people couldn't delete computer files.

Lucie eyed the hallway in front of her. The front door. Her way out. *Just leave.*

She should go. Get out of this crazy situation and go back to her office. Back to running Coco Barknell.

Ro.

Lucie pulled her gaze from the door to Lorraine, still standing near the study entrance.

"Get out," Lorraine said.

Lucie met her cold stare. "I'm going. I have a question first."

"Fine. What?"

"Why did you delete that backup?"

16

———

*R*UN.

Something inside, deep in Lucie's brain, screamed it. *Run. Run. Run.* She eyed the front door again. Probably locked. But she had a straight shot. Even if Lorraine cut through the study, Lucie would get the jump on her.

What was she running from? She'd yet to figure out what had happened. Maybe someone else, one of Buzzy's legion of assistants deleted that file.

Except, Lorraine wasn't denying it. Lucie had asked her straight out.

"Don't fucking do it! 5511! Piss off!"

Lorraine screwed up her face and stomped toward Felix. "Shut the fuck up!"

Oh, boy. Looney Lorraine.

"I've been listening to that bird night and day since my sister died. He never stops. It's constant. Now I'm done."

Lucie had a flash of panic, a vision of Felix, his little claws clinging to his perch as Lorraine swung that cage in a fit of rage.

Nuh-uh. If nothing else, Lucie would save a defenseless

bird. In honor of Ro, whom she'd failed, she'd save the PITA bird.

She caught up to Lorraine and elbowed around her, forming a human shield in front of Felix's cage.

She worked up her best Lucie sneer and put a little mean into it. "Don't you touch him. He's grieving. And, and...he's pissed because he saw—"

Whoopsie. Couldn't say that. Saying that equaled throwing bloody bait into shark infested waters.

Lorraine faced her again, her eyes hyper-focused and burning. "He saw her die. *I* know. But it was an accident."

Lucie's head snapped back.

An *accident.* Again, Lucie eyed the exit. What the hell had she gotten herself into?

"Sure," she said. "I get it. It's not Felix's fault though. Let's just stay calm here."

"I'm calm. Trust me. After the week I've had, I'm an expert at calm. Now is no exception." Lorraine took one step forward. "We have a problem, Lucie."

Problem? What problem? No problem.

Run.

Lucie pointed over her shoulder to the door. "If you're okie-dokey here, I'll just—"

Lorraine's hand whipped out, locking on Lucie's arm.

Well, apparently they were going *there.*

Lucie backed farther into the room, bumped a side chair, and, with Lorraine's hold tightening, slid sideways. The chair held two throw pillows. Fairly useless weapons, but a girl had to work with what she had. She reached down, gripped a corner of one of the pillows, and something in Lorraine's crazy eyes flashed.

Ffffttt. Lucie whipped the pillow, yanked free of the viselike grip, and bolted, her feet gaining traction on the area rug.

Front door. Right there. Just feet away.

Oooofff! Something slammed into her, a huge blast of weight that rocked her. The tablet flew as Lucie went airborne, her body hurling forward, crashing into the couch and jarring her shoulder.

Ignoring the pain, she rolled to her back, and found Lorraine getting to her feet after that tackle fit for the Bears defensive line. She leaped and Lucie started swinging, her bunched hands sliding off Lorraine's shoulders and arms.

Hey, no one ever said she rivaled Muhammad Ali. Ro had always been the brawler.

"Stupid," Lorraine said. "You couldn't mind your own damned business. It was an accident."

Lorraine reared back, cocking a fist, and Lucie bucked—hard—knocking her off balance, then bucking again to finish the job. Lorraine tipped sideways, half rolling off and leaving Lucie use of her left leg. She kicked out, did a weird shimmy-kick-shimmy routine, and managed to shove the lunatic off.

Now this bitch is mine.

Lucie bounced to her feet, jumped on her attacker and grabbed two fistfuls of hair.

"Aaaaaa!" Lorraine screamed. "Get off me."

A huge *bam* sounded from the entry way and the front door flew open. Tim burst through, weapon drawn, and something in Lucie's chest exploded.

Thank God, he's here. Her man.

"Off," he shouted in his cop voice.

Lucie put her hands up.

"I didn't do anything. It's her. I think she killed her sister. The parrot saw the whole thing."

"DON'T MOVE," TIM SHOUTED AS RELIEF, THAT ENORMOUS release of pressure, flew from his shoulders.

That moment of panic when he'd heard the screaming probably took what was left of his stomach and an additional few years from his life.

And here was peanut Lucie, beating the crap out of Buzzy's sister.

Not bothering to listen, Lorraine shoved at Lucie. "Get off me."

"Luce," Tim said. "Off."

How many freaking times had he said that to her in the last months? Somehow, in her never-ending quest to right wrongs, she always wound up jumping someone. He'd give her credit for being fearless.

She rolled to her feet, taking a fighter's stance, ready to pounce again if necessary. Unbelievable.

Tim jerked his head at Lorraine. "On your feet."

"This is absurd."

"I'm sure it is." In his mood, if she tried anything, he'd lock her up for aggravating him.

Two armed detectives hustled into the house, spotted him, and stopped short.

"Tim O'Brien," he said, angling so they could see the badge hooked on his belt.

Tim didn't know them, but assumed they were the lead detectives on the Sneider case.

The female detective stepped forward, holstered her weapon and badged him. "We talked to your lieutenant. Whatcha got?"

"This is Lorraine Sneider, sister of Buzzy Sneider, and

Lucie Rizzo. I walked in and found the two of them wrestling it out. I just got them up off the floor."

"Thanks," the other detective said.

The female detective, Sorenson, stepped toward Lorraine. "I need to pat you down, do you have any weapons on you? Anything in your pockets?"

Lorraine gasped. "Of course not."

She gave her a cursory pat down then turned to Lucie, who still had her hands up. Tim nearly laughed.

After ascertaining the ladies weren't carrying, the detective sat them both on opposite chairs. Lorraine on the sofa and Lucie in a side chair. Sorenson took the remaining seat. Her partner wandered toward the kitchen, looking all around as he went. Tim stayed near the door, out of the action.

"All right," Sorenson said, "what happened here?"

Lorraine jumped right in. "I caught her snooping on my sister's tablet. Isn't that invasion of privacy or something? I want her arrested."

"Hey," Lucie said, "I was trying to find a security video from the night of the murder. I'd think you'd want to know who killed your sister. *Apparently* not."

Lorraine gritted her teeth and Lucie made a zipping motion across her lips.

Sorenson raised her hands. "Ladies, please. Ms. Sneider, let's start with this security video."

"I don't know anything about it."

Tim wasn't going for that. She had to know something. Who else but the closest family members would have access to Buzzy's personal affairs? Well, other than the army of assistants.

Lucie cut her eyes to Lorraine. "*Someone* deleted it."

Sorenson exchanged a look with Tim. He sympathized,

but this wasn't his first Lucie rodeo. So he just shrugged and kept his mouth shut.

The detective faced Lucie again. "How do you know?"

"Mmmm, well, because I logged into Buzzy's account. I mean, I know I shouldn't have, but Lorraine was busy and I had the password for the tablet. I wanted to see if the backup was there."

The fact that Lucie had the password for the tablet seemed to surprise Sorenson. Hell, it surprised Tim—and that was saying something. After months with the Rizzo crew, he'd become hardened to shock factor.

Sorenson jumped all over that. "Why did you have the password?"

"Felix gave it to me."

"Who's Felix?"

"Don't fucking do it! 5511! Piss off!"

The squawk brought Tim around to the cage sitting by the window. Who'd have thought such a small bird would have such a projectable voice?

"I hate that bird," Lorraine said. "He's been screaming at me for days."

Lucie jabbed a finger at the cage. "He *saw* something. 5511 is the password for the tablet. That's how I knew to try it. When I logged in, the video from the day Buzzy died was the only one missing."

Her face twisted into that scrunched-up look of determination Tim had fallen in love with. But a parrot witness? Even for her, a stretch.

"You shut up!"

Whoa, now. Lorraine getting uppity. Tim shifted sideways, closer to Lucie, in case another smack down ensued.

"I won't shut up. I've been to Buzzy's house and she kept

Felix in the same room where—" Lucie rolled one hand. "—you know. That poor bird is a *witness.*"

Sorenson sighed. "What a freak show."

Her partner entered the room and scooped the tablet off the floor. "I got the tablet."

Lorraine's eyes shot to the device, then to the detective's gloved hands, and her Adam's apple bobbed.

"Don't fucking do it! 5511! Piss off! Don't fucking do it! 5511! Piss off! Don't fucking do it! 5511! Piss off!"

"Oh, God." Lorraine pressed her palms into her eyes and held them there as she rocked forward.

The room went silent, all the remaining players refusing to move or speak because, in Tim's experience, escalating tension made things happen. Made people talk when they should stay silent.

Come on, Lorraine, start yapping.

"Don't fucking do it! 5511! Piss off! Don't fucking do it! 5511! Piss off!"

"Lorraine," Sorenson said, above the squawk, "are you all right?"

The woman sat perched on the edge of her seat, her arms tucked around her middle, rocking back and forth, back and forth, back and forth. A tight band of tension snapped at the back of Tim's neck.

Sensing something, Sorenson scooted closer. "You know, it's been a tough week. You've been cooperative with us since this started. Is there anything you'd like to add?"

"Don't fucking do it! 5511! Piss off!"

Lorraine's shoulders dropped, just absolutely fell, as the energy and fight seemed to leave her body. Tim glanced at Lucie, the two of them exchanging a bewildered look. If she didn't keep her mouth shut, he might have to kill her. Or himself. Finally end the misery.

"I don't know," Lorraine said.

"About what?"

Lorraine snorted. "Everything." She met Sorenson's gaze and tears bubbled in her eyes. "My sister is dead."

"I know. I'm sorry."

"It was an accident."

An accident. She knew something. *This is it.* Tim stood stock still, fighting the brutal assault of energy plowing into him. This wasn't his case, but damn he wanted to jump in. Hop all over this woman and get some answers before she lawyered up.

"All right," Sorenson said, her voice even and controlled. "Can you tell me about it?"

A few seconds of quiet ensued until Lorraine shook her head and let out breathy sigh that screamed of exhaustion. "We were...tipsy," she said. "Celebrating the sales of the Coco Barknell designs." She turned her head to Lucie. "I'm sorry, by the way. I really am. We did steal them. With all the press about the fashion show, Buzzy wanted to strike while things were hot. She thought she could make a deal with you after the fact. It was a timing thing."

Giving up on his quest to appear unfazed, Tim rolled his eyes. *A timing thing. Right.*

Sorenson rose from her chair and sat on the coffee table in front of Lorraine, cocking her head in that sympathetic way women did when talking their friends off a ledge. "I know this is difficult for you. She was your sister. Accidents happen all the time. What happened? You said you were drunk."

Lorraine nodded, wiped her drippy nose with her hand. "Yes. Buzzy left the office early and told me to meet her at the house. When I arrived, she'd already downed half a bottle of wine. By the time we finished the second bottle, we were giggly and got on the subject of how I used to give her wedgies all the time. We laughed about it. I thought it would be funny to wedgie her." Lorraine splayed her fingers wide and put her hands out. "I swear that's all I was doing. Being funny."

"Understandable," Sorenson said. "What happened?"

"I grabbed the waistband of her underwear and yanked, you know? Just sort of tugging. We were laughing so hard because it wasn't going well, and that made us laugh harder. The more I yanked, the more her feet came off the floor and we were just...being stupid. Buzzy started screaming. She kept saying 'Don't fucking do it! Don't fucking do it!' but she was laughing. And so was I. We were having fun."

Without moving her head, Lucie slid her gaze to Tim. Holy hell, not only was the parrot a witness, he'd just helped them solve this case.

"Then what happened?"

"Stupid wine. I never could hold my liquor. I pulled her underwear so hard, I knocked her off balance and she fell." Lorraine cuffed herself on the head. "She hit her head on the edge of that enormous marble table she has."

That explained the head trauma. Tim hadn't seen the criminologist's report and the brass wasn't sharing details, but he suspected Sorenson knew something about what had clubbed Buzzy on the head. Using the size and shape of the head wound as a guide, forensic pathologists would have determined possible weapons.

"Did it knock her out?"

"I guess. She fell over." Lorraine's mouth dipped at the corners and she closed her eyes. "I thought she was goofing around. She used to do that when we were kids. She'd pretend to be asleep and then leap up and attack me. While she was on the ground, I gave her the wedgie. Pulled it way up."

Lorraine pounded her fists against her head, tears now sliding over her cheeks. "I thought I was being funny. You know, doing an atomic wedgie."

Tim forced himself not to look at Lucie. Homicide by atomic wedgie.

Only in Lucie's world could *that* happen.

"I was too drunk to realize she wasn't pretending to be asleep. After teasing her, I put my head back for a second and passed out. I swear, when I fell asleep the waistband was on her head. She must have woken up or moved or something. I don't know. But I didn't put it around her neck. I wouldn't have done that. I loved her."

Lucie produced a wad of tissues from her pocket. *No, don't.* Tim gritted his teeth. Helluva time for Lucie to be thoughtful. He adored her for it, but she'd kill the momentum and...too late.

She handed the tissues to Lorraine. "They're clean."

"Thank you. You really are a nice person. I'm sorry I broke into your shop and ruined all those samples."

"*You* did that?"

Lorraine squeezed her eyes closed. "I panicked. I knew you were asking questions and thought I could scare you off."

Sorenson shot Lucie a look then went back to Lorraine. "We'll get to that later. Tell us about Buzzy. You passed out and then what?"

"I woke up to the doorbell ringing and Felix screaming."

The doorbell. That must have been Roseanne.

"I came out of my stupor and saw the underwear around her neck." Lorraine touched her throat, gliding her fingers over her skin. "She must not have been able to tear it off. I panicked, cut the underwear off and called 911, but it was too late. By the time they got there, she was gone."

Lorraine looked over at Lucie. "You were right. While I was waiting for the ambulance, I freaked. I dumped the wine bottles, put the glasses in the dishwasher, and...deleted the video from Buzzy's account. I was scared and under the influence and made a stupid decision. Then I remembered the online backup and deleted that one too." She went back to Sorenson. "I killed my sister."

"That dirty, lying witch," Lucie said.

She stood next to Tim's car, hands on hips, fuming over the injustice while detectives loaded Lorraine into their vehicle.

Poor Ro had been arrested and subjected to scrutiny and now, Lucie knew, even with Lorraine's confession, the story would probably never go away. It was too big. Too juicy. A famous reality star and an *associate* of the Rizzo crime family. It had made-for-television-movie all over it.

"Yep," Tim agreed. "Fear makes people do crazy things."

"So, not only did they steal Ro's work, Lorraine would have let her go to prison to save her own butt. And she almost got away with it." She shook her head. "I don't get people. How is this world so crazy?"

Tim faced her, his fair cheeks red from the cold, and set his hands on her shoulders. "Eventually, it would have come out. That missing video was a red flag. The detectives would have narrowed that down."

"Still, the deceit. It's horrible."

"Yes, it is."

"And she had the nerve to organize that protest to make people believe Ro was guilty."

He pulled her close, kissing the top of her head. She breathed in, snuggling against him for a few seconds, taking it all in. The comfort, the solid foundation he provided when her world blew apart. And after the week they'd had, she welcomed it.

She tilted her head back and smiled. "Thank you for that. I was afraid you were mad at me."

He shrugged. "I'll admit, you're slowly killing me. I get it though. And you know what this means, right?"

Oh, she knew. She'd been through enough trials with her father to understand the intricacies of cases that fell apart. "Ro will be released."

"Yep."

The detectives drove off and Lucie let out a long sigh. She needed a nap. A three-day one.

Her phone rang, reminding her she needed to start calling people. In the time her phone had been shut off, she'd missed twenty-three calls. Eight of them from Tim.

The rest—business calls—she'd return later. First, she needed to reach Joey, Ro's parents, Mom and Dad, the Cock Heads. Everyone who'd helped should be told the news.

Roseanne would be coming home.

"I think I'll throw a party when she gets out. At the store. She'll love the attention."

"You're a good friend, Luce."

She shrugged. "I love her."

Her gaze went to the front door, now being boarded up since Tim had wrecked it when he kicked it in. And how hot was that? Her man, the beast.

"Wait," she said. "What about Felix?"

"The parrot?"

"Yes. I think he's still in there. Someone has to take care of him."

"If a family member doesn't want him, I guess he'll go to a shelter."

Oh, she couldn't have that. Felix was a hero. An unlikely one, but a hero.

"I want him."

Tim snorted. "Right. I can see that in the Rizzo house. Are you *kidding* me?"

"I'll make it work. He helped clear Ro. I owe it to him."

"You think your mom wants that loudmouth in her house? I mean, no offense, she's already got her hands full with your dad."

At that, Lucie laughed. "True." She thought it through for a second. Felix in Villa Rizzo would be a disaster. He was too loud and they'd never get any sleep. Mom didn't deserve that.

The store though. She'd keep him there. People were in and out of there all day so he'd get plenty of attention. And hopefully he wouldn't drive them crazy with the squawking. She had to try.

"I'll keep him at Coco Barknell. He'll be a symbol of all that we accomplished together." She snuggled into him again. "All of us."

Tim nodded. "I think you're crazy, but I see your point."

"Can I take him?"

"Now?"

"Someone has to until they figure out where he'll wind up."

Tim smiled and the stress and exhaustion of the last days slid right off her. Somehow, they'd managed to get through this without demolishing the boundaries of Tim's job.

"I do love you, Luce."

"I love you too. I hope you know that."

"Yeah, I do." He pointed at the house. "I'll go in and get you a loudmouth bird."

AT 7:08 P.M. ROSEANNE, IN HER USUAL DRAMATIC FASHION, swung open the door to Coco Barknell, hanging on as it moved, her body angling on her stiletto heels.

The sight of her in her tight skirt—maybe not as tight as a few days ago—and blouse with the extra button undone made Lucie smile.

Her pal was back. Boobs and all.

"Luuuucie," Ro yelled in her best Ricky Ricardo accent. "I'm home."

"Luuuucie," Felix responded. "I'm home."

Lawdy. If he decided that would be his new tagline, it would make for some long days.

Joey followed Ro in, shaking his head. "That parrot has to go."

Eh. Who cared as long as they were all together?

Lucie hopped up from her chair and rushed toward her BFF, arms at the ready for the hug of all hugs. "Welcome back." Maybe she said that a tad louder than necessary, but she needed to trigger the crew huddled in the break room.

Any second now, they'd pour into the hallway, charging toward the guest of honor. Ro would love it. All her people in one place.

Fawning over her.

A dream come true.

"Surprise!" All at once the hallway filled with bodies—Ro parents and extended family, Lucie's as well, the crew from Petey's, Tim, the Cock Heads—each of them battling for space and bouncing off each other in the narrow area.

A wide smile stretched across Ro's face. She slapped her hands over her chest, batting her eyes. "What? For me?"

The Queen of all Things Fabulous on her triumphant return.

"Yes, for you," Lucie said. "You've got a big mouth, but we missed you."

"Big mouth," Felix said.

Ro's mom and dad rushed forward, her mother throwing her arms up. "My baby!"

"Here we go again," Lucie's mom muttered.

Lucie stepped back, out of the line of fire, before Mrs. B. mowed her over.

Mr. B. followed, wrapping his arms around both of them. "My girls."

Lucie's chest locked up and she forced a breath. Of all the screwy situations she'd been involved in these past months, nothing compared to this one. To possibly losing Ro. The full brunt of it, the heavy weight of that loss, finally hit her.

"Don't fucking do it! 5511! Piss off!"

Felix's rant momentarily silenced the room, but then a cheer went out, everyone clapping for their unlikely hero. Ro peeled away from the crowd and walked to the cage, tapping her finger on it.

"Hey, little man," she said, "thank you."

The bird cocked his head, stared at Ro with his black little eyes and squawked. "Vaffanculo!"

Beside Lucie, Jimmy Two-Toes winced and she growled at him for what had to be the tenth time.

"Ohmygod," Ro said. "Did this little turd just tell me to go F myself? In *Italian*?"

Ohmygod was right. Lucie had let dad's crazy crew take Felix to Petey's for an hour while she got everything for the party set up, and look what happened.

Lucie whirled, flapping her arms. "Jimmy! Stop teaching him that stuff."

"Sorry, Luce. But, you know, it's handy sometimes."

Ro turned back to the crowd. "Who'd have thought this little guy would help get me out of the clink? Only the best for him now."

Mom held up her hands. "Everyone, in the kitchen. Food is ready."

Good old Mom. Always handling the big appetites. Lucie had wanted to cater this shin-dig, but Mom wouldn't hear of it. She loved Ro like her own. No store bought food would do for this occasion.

While Ro was processed out of the county lockup, Mom whipped up a feast for forty. An assignment not a lot of women could handle.

Ro went straight to Mom, squeezing her into a hug. "Thank you. This is the best homecoming ever."

"You know I'm happy to do it," Mom said. "This was special. I made your favorite mousse cake. It was a rush job, though, so I'm not promising it'll be any good."

Ro backed away from the hug. "It'll be perfect. Did I mention I think I lost a few pounds while in jail?"

And it begins...

While the crowd shuffled into the break room, Tim wandered up next to Lucie and dropped an arm over her shoulder. "How long do you think it'll take her to weigh herself?"

"At least until she gets home. I ditched the scale she had hidden in the supply closet. I wouldn't be surprised if she stopped at the jail's infirmary to check before she left."

"Women."

Lucie tipped her head up and grinned. "It's oddly comforting. I've missed her." She tugged on his suit jacket. "Thank you for helping. That battle with Lorraine may not have ended well for me if you hadn't busted in there."

"Luce, believe me, I've seen you in action. You're small, but mighty. You'd have taken her."

Oh, way to work a girl. She went up on tip-toes and kissed his cheek. "And can I tell you? That whole kicking in the door thing? H-O-T. If all goes well here, you'll get lucky tonight, detective."

Behind them, the doggie bells jangled and Frankie rushed in. A weird pulsing seized her stomach.

"Damn," he said, staring at the crowd huddled in the hallway. "She's here already? I missed it?"

Lucie straightened her shoulders, making sure not to pull too far from Tim. Months of conversation had clued her in to his vulnerabilities over Frankie, and he needed to know he was her guy.

"You're fine," Lucie said. "She got here a few minutes ago."

"Freaking traffic."

He strode toward them in his usual confident Frankie style and held his hand to Tim. The two men shook and that odd pulsing kicked in again.

This was...weird. Only word for it.

"Hi, Frankie," Tim said. "Good to see you."

Oh, boy.

"Lucie." Ro appeared in the doorway leading to the kitchen area. "You need to eat."

She spotted Frankie, let out a scream that should have cracked the ceiling, and charged. Hips swinging, boobs bouncing, hair flying. Ro. In the flesh. All of it made Lucie smile.

Over the years, Ro and Frankie's relationship could best be described as...intense. They took pride in harassing each other and one-upping snide comments. But down deep? Love. Camaraderie.

"Charm boy!" Ro threw her arms around him, knocking him back a full step. "What are you doing here?"

"Please," he said, "you in lockup? I wasn't missing that. Hell, I may write a book and make millions off you."

"Vaffanculo," Felix wailed.

Frankie cracked up. "Who the hell taught him that?"

"Jimmy. Who do you think?"

"Unbelievable."

"I know," Ro said. "And he totally used it in context, because that's *exactly* what I was thinking."

But she was smiling and so was Frankie. It brought Lucie—and her emotions—back. Back to when she and Frankie were, well, Lucie and Frankie. The dream team the neighborhood thought would get married and pop out a bunch of babies.

Except perfect wasn't so perfect. Now here they were, Frankie living half a country away and Lucie cuddled up with Tim.

While Frankie and Ro had their reunion, Lucie glanced up at her handsome Irish detective. He watched her, his look flat-lipped and pensive.

"You okay?" she asked.

"Me? Fine. You?"

She bumped him with her shoulder. "I'm great."

Tim didn't look like he believed it.

"Luce," Ro said, "come on. Let's eat. I've been fed gruel

for three days. I swear I'll never complain about your mother making me fat again."

Ha. That'd be the day. "As if I believe that?"

But Lucie let Ro thread her arm through hers and lead her toward the break room. She glanced over her shoulder at Frankie and Tim. "You boys coming?"

Tim hung back.

In the two times he'd seen Frankie since the drama of Buzzy's death began, he'd had been nothing but respectful. Still, palpable tension couldn't be denied.

Frankie stood in front of Felix's cage, lightly tapping on it. "This guy will fit right in around here. Hard to believe he gave Lucie the password to that tablet."

Ah, so Frankie knew about that. Had Lucie told him? Or Joey? Tim wanted to believe the information came from Joey. Really, he'd be happy if Lucie never talked to Frankie again.

Crappy? Yes. He didn't care. He wanted all of Lucie, and Frankie's presence distracted her. She'd never admitted it, but Tim sensed it. The way her mind drifted in Frankie's presence, the distance and confusion. Heavy baggage, that.

Frankie gave up on the bird and turned to Tim. "You know I love her, right?"

No doubt who the "her" in that statement was.

"There's a lot to love. You know *I* love her, right?"

Frankie sighed. "I do now." He propped himself on the edge of Ro's desk and crossed his arms. "I'd hoped it wasn't serious between you two. Easy to do from New York. I asked her to come with me and keep hoping she'll change her mind."

What Frankie expected Tim to say, he wasn't sure. He kept it simple and stayed silent.

"She wanted to stay here," Frankie said. "All that time she'd begged me to leave Franklin and she winds up staying. Go figure."

Following the other man's lead, Tim sat on the edge of Lucie's desk, resting his hands at his sides, the two of them literally faced off across the aisle. "She has a dream for this place. Knows what she wants. She couldn't leave the business or the employees."

"I know." A simple agreement.

No pissing match here. Just two guys in love with the same woman.

Tim jerked his thumb to the right. "She keeps the Fortune 500 logo taped to the inside of her desk drawer. Says it keeps her motivated."

Frankie laughed. "That's her."

For a minute, he stared down at his shoes, more than likely considering where he wanted to take this conversation. Tim? Considering he hadn't started this, he'd wait Frankie out.

Eventually, Frankie stood. "I'm not giving up on her. We've broken up and gotten back together more times than we can count. We always find our way back."

Never one to let a man assume the power position, Tim stood and met Frankie's eye. "In the past, yes. Now? Don't be too sure. I'm not going anywhere."

"I guess we're both clear on it then."

Tim stepped forward and extended his hand. Frankie accepted the gesture, the two of them shaking hands in that age-old competitive way that let the other know a bloody brawl would ensue.

Well, Frankie could bring it on. Tim was sure as hell not giving Lucie up without a fight.

By 11:00 p.m., the party animals, having had an abundance of good food and entertainment ala Felix, all left the shop in search of their beds. Lucie couldn't blame them. She loved her friends and family, but as a whole they were high-maintenance.

At least Jimmy had given up teaching Felix Italian swear words, opting instead for Vic Damone songs.

A day in the life of Lucie Rizzo.

She glanced over at the conference table where Tim sat in one of the cushy leather chairs, head back and eyes closed. Poor guy was beat.

Ro emerged from the break room with Joey on her heels, his eyes glued to her rear. "Listen," he said, "don't take too long. I gotta talk to Frankie for a few minutes and then we're leaving. It was a bitch of a week and I'm tired."

Ro flapped her hand at him. "Blah, blah. I've been locked up for days. We'll go when I'm ready."

Ah, yes. Normalcy. A beautiful thing.

Ro paused at her desk as Joey marched out the shop door. She let out a laugh. "He thinks *he's* had a rough week?"

Lucie smiled. "Now that you're back, he's re-establishing his boundaries."

"Ha! I'll give him boundaries." Ro's lips quirked as she stared through the glass where Joey and Frankie stood on the sidewalk. Joey and Ro. A match made in heaven.

"Hey," Lucie said, "when you're done mooning over my brother, I need to discuss something with you."

"Should I leave?" Tim asked. "I can wait outside."

"No. You can hear this."

Ro straightened the pencil cup on her desk, then fiddled with the stapler and tape dispenser before sitting down. "It feels so good to be home and talking to you. You have no idea."

"It's great to have you back."

"What did you want to talk to me about?"

"The stolen designs."

"Ugh. Way to ruin my mood."

Good old Ro. "No. It's okay. Before Lorraine went psycho on me today, we chatted about your designs."

"The ones those thieving bitches stole?"

From his spot at the conference table, Tim sighed. Who could blame him?

"Yes. Those. Lorraine offered us a fifty-fifty revenue split on sales. Plus, Coco Barknell would get full design credit. I'm assuming, even with everything that's gone on, she'll keep her word because we can still ruin their reputation."

Ro sat back and pursed her lips. The skeptical face. *"Really."*

"Yes. Really."

"But they're not admitting they're thieving bitches?"

"Uh, no. Sorry."

When it came to Buzzy and receiving justice, Ro might never be satisfied. In Lucie's mind? Growing their business with the help of Buzzy's—God rest her soul—marketing power might be the best form of justice around.

Ro twisted her lips one way, then the other. "Well, what do you think?"

"Remember, I'm the numbers person. Are you sure you want my opinion?"

Snoring noises ensued. How was it possible Lucie had missed all this?

"You think we should do it."

"It stinks that they stole our—*your*—designs. I don't know that either of us will ever feel good about that. We need to find the upside, though, and I think the volume of sales we'd get by partnering with Buzzy's company will be exorbitantly more than we'd get on our own. At this juncture anyway. Add the name recognition, and—aside from them being thieving beyotches—I can't find a lot wrong with it."

Ro opened her mouth and Lucie held her hand up. "I'm not done. *I* may not mind this deal, but they're your designs. They stole them from *you*. If you want, we'll walk away and either sue them, or demand the designs back."

"You'd do that?"

Without question. Lucie had spent the whole of her adult life letting her father's lifestyle eat away at her. Little by little, like acid in her belly, tearing her apart while she plastered on a pleasant face and disregarded the devastating rumors and whispers. As much as she wanted to believe she'd been able to ignore it all, it came with a price. An angry price. One she didn't want Ro to pay. "Roseanne, I love you. I want you to be happy. Absolutely, without a doubt, I'll support whatever decision you make."

Ro blinked a few times then swiveled her chair sideways. "O'Hottie, what do you think?"

Later, Lucie would give Ro a giant smooch and maybe even kiss her Gucci-clad feet for including him. As much as he refused to admit it, Frankie's appearance this week had rattled him. Outside of reassuring Tim that she loved him, she wasn't sure how to make the Frankie issue disappear.

Frankie would always have a place in her heart. Didn't mean she'd throw Tim over for him.

Tim tilted his head one way then the other. "If it were

me, based on the plans you two have for growing the business, the marketing aspects of a partnership with Buzzy's company alone could take you to the next level. I'd take the fifty percent and get ready to cash checks."

A loud knock sounded against the glass. Joey. Ape man ready to leave.

"Now he's rushing me?" Ro shot out of her chair and poked a finger at him. "Quit banging and go slap yourself."

Her brother laughed. Laughed.

Idiot.

These two. Perfect for each other.

"Think about it," Lucie said. "We have time. Lorraine certainly isn't going anywhere."

Ro grabbed her coat from the fancy coat rack she'd put in the corner near her desk. "No. Make the deal. Let's just get this done with. After the hell of this week, I want a fresh start. Besides, I have plenty more designs we can capitalize on."

Whoot! Lucie envisioned a small mountain of money. All that happy green stuff piling up. Hot-diggity-dog. If this deal went the way she hoped, Ro would get more than a raise. She'd get a partnership. A stake in Coco Barknell. True partners. Something that meant more than a silly raise. A partnership represented love and trust and...faith. In Ro.

All things Lucie had in spades.

"I'll make the deal," she said.

Joey shoved the door open, sending the doggie bells jingling. "Sometime today?"

"Oh, I'm coming. Keep your shorts on."

He held his hand out. A sweet and un-Joey like gesture that indicated there might be hope for him. Her brother. The mush.

Tim blew out a hard breath. "Gotta say, as weird as they are, it works."

"I know. If I think too long about it, my head will explode."

Tim laughed. "Are you ready to go? Want to clean up the back before we leave?"

They'd sent all the food home with various people and had washed whatever dishes needed tending, but the break room required straightening. Folding table broken down, paper products stored, a good sweep. She just didn't have it in her to do it tonight. "Nah. I'll do it tomorrow. I think I promised my man he might get lucky."

"Wow. You're going to leave that mess? For me?"

Always. "When it comes to you, O'Hottie, you'd better believe it."

"Luce?"

"Yes?"

"I talked to Frankie."

"About?"

"You." He put his hands up. "He started it. You know me. I don't talk about us to anyone without your okay. He wanted me to know he still loves you."

Oh, Frankie. How many different ways could he break her heart?

In the four years they'd been a couple, heartbreak on both sides had been continuous. They'd run the gamut of emotions. Ups and downs aplenty.

With Tim? None of that. Just fun. And laughter. And great sex with a guy who gave her tingles every time she got within ten feet.

"I see," she said. "What did you say?"

"I let him know that I loved you too." He leaned down and kissed her, a slow brush of his lips that curled her toes.

He backed away and smiled. "I also told him I wasn't going anywhere. That is, of course, unless you send me packing."

She gripped his jacket, yanked him down for another kiss. "No way, O'Hottie. I'm not setting you loose. Who else could put up with the nonsense my life entails?"

"You *are* slowly killing me."

"I know. I'm sorry."

He draped an arm over her shoulder and started for the door. "Don't be. Before you, my life was boring. I kinda like this newfound adventure that comes with loving Lucie Rizzo."

They reached the door and Lucie slapped the light switch on the inside wall, drenching the shop in darkness.

Her place. Her man.

Life as Lucie Rizzo, mob princess, was looking up.

EXCERPT OF COOKED

BY USA TODAY BESTSELLING AUTHOR ADRIENNE GIORDANO

Book five in The Lucie Rizzo Mystery series:

ON A GRAY JANUARY DAY IN CHICAGO, LUCIE RIZZO SHOVED her shop's door closed, blocking out the frigid wind as Coco Barknell's potential future headed down the sidewalk. At her feet, Jimmy Two-Toes' mangy Jack Russell terrier, Sonny, licked his chops.

"Did you see this dog devour that food? Look at him. He'd sell his soul for another shot at that marinated chicken. We should jump on this."

Lucie's business partner and all-around BFF, Roseanne, sat at her desk, her sexy-librarian reading glasses perched on her nose.

"That dog," she said, eyes still on her monitor, "was a half-starved stray when Jimmy found him. He'd sell his soul for gruel. *Not* a good barometer."

The clunk of the furnace echoed through the large room that had once been Carlucci's shoe store. For years, Lucie's mom had bought their shoes in this very place. Now it housed Lucie's growing dog-walking and upscale pet accessory business.

Lucie waved Ro off. "Please. Jimmy found him a year ago. He's over that starving, desperate dog phase. And have you seen what he eats? Raw steak. Filets for crying out loud. He's *evolved*."

"*Vafanculo!*" Felix squawked and Lucie let out a long sigh.

She'd rescued the feisty parrot after his owner died, and her mob-boss father's cronies enjoyed teaching the little guy Italian swear words. Words Lucie and Ro had to hear all day.

All.

Day.

"Pipe down, Felix."

"Pipe down, Felix," the bird repeated.

Ro snorted and rolled her eyes, but Lucie didn't have time for arguing. No sir. She marched back to her desk, swiveled her chair, and dropped into it.

Instinct, in Lucie's twenty-seven years, had served her well. Right now, every nerve ending tingled and that normally quiet voice in her head boomed like a Bruce Springsteen concert.

In front of her sat a jar of Jo-Jo's Pride, the dog food sample that Sonny, a street-hardened warrior, would chew off Lucie's arm for. Sonny leaped straight up, his head clearing the top of the desk.

"Down!"

But Sonny, as evolved as his palate might be, like his owner, didn't take orders well. *Did he just swing his snout to that jar?*

Lucie pointed. "Did you see that?"

"What?"

"He pointed at the jar with his snout."

Ro laughed and flipped her long sable hair over her shoulder, the fat thank-you-curling-iron curls flying. How was it that beautiful women pulled that move off so effortlessly, while women like Lucie—petite, Mary Average women—looked like idiots?

"He did not," Ro said. "You're just saying that to get me to agree to this crazy partnership idea."

True. But the dog had done it.

"Ro, we have to get in on this deal."

"We don't know diddly about manufacturing dog food. And, hello, Jo-Jo Flowers? She was a space cadet in high school. What does she know about creating a dog food line?"

"She knows enough to make $100,000 in eighteen months." Lucie picked up the jar. "With the right partners and marketing, this stuff is a gold mine."

Ro slid her glasses to the edge of her nose and stared at

Lucie over the rim. "It's way—*way*—outside our comfort zone."

Pfft. Whatever. "Ten months ago, so was doggie apparel. Look at us now? We have a major department store account —thanks to you—and our own e-commerce website. In less than a year we're seeing a profit. A small one, sure, but still. And, hello, I was an investment banker. I can hook us up with the right people. This is a no-brainer."

Ro went back to her computer. "It takes us from our core business."

"That's what you're worried about?"

"Darned straight. We're building a brand and you want to deviate from that."

"Our brand is high-end dog items. You don't think a dog food company that lets you custom order your own mix of flavors is high-end?"

Lucie scooped up the jar and walked to Ro's desk with Sonny doing that crazy leap as he followed her. She set the jar down and Sonny bounced up again.

"That jumping makes me nuts," Ro said.

"It's a Jack Russell thing. Jimmy said he can clear a five-foot fence."

Lucie glanced down at him and he bared his teeth. Smiling. At least Jimmy called it smiling. Lucie wasn't quite sure. Every time he did it though, Jimmy tossed him a piece of beef jerky. Whatever this teeth-baring thing was, the dog meant no harm. He was just jonesing for a treat.

She bent down and tickled him under the chin. "You're a scroungey looking thing, but you're cute."

He nudged his head toward the desk and shifted his eyes back to her.

"Look at him. Total man-slut for this food right now." She leaned in, offered up her cheek, and Sonny swiped his tongue over it. "Good boy. And since I'm a sucker, I'll give you the rest of this food. Just don't tell your daddy. You know he's watching your calories."

Ro pushed out of her chair, straightened her silk blouse, and did that strutting walk of hers to retrieve the bowl Sonny cleaned on his first round.

Before the remaining chicken and lamb hit the bowl, Sonny was in motion, shoving his snout right under Lucie's hand.

Ro stood by, tapping one stiletto clad foot. "I don't know, Luce. This scares me."

"Why?"

She gestured to the garment rack holding her latest design samples, all handmade for various sizes of dogs. Everything from Chihuahuas to Great Danes. "What we do, we can produce ourselves. We have a team of seamstresses that help us, yes, but it doesn't take a huge distribution plant. What you're talking about is a food product. The standards will be different. We'd have to partner with a large-scale processing plant. Which is exactly why Jo-Jo hasn't been able to grow this business. She said it herself."

"That's *not* what she said. The small factories can't handle the demand, but the bigger ones require more orders than she currently has. Without additional capital, she simply can't afford to expand. She's needs a backer. With my banking contacts, that's a problem I can fix—for a cut of the profits. It's a win-win."

Ro tossed her glasses on the desk and peered down at Sonny, who licked the bowl clean. "It's your company."

Really, it wasn't. Not anymore. The papers were still with the lawyer, but based on Ro's performance over the past year, Lucie had decided to give her BFF a fifteen percent share of Coco Barknell.

"Actually," Lucie said, "I need to talk to you about that."

"Uh-oh. I swear, Lucie Rizzo, if you tell me you've sold this company I will kill you where you stand. I will bury your body where it'll never be found."

Want more? Don't miss the next Lucie Rizzo mystery.

A NOTE TO READERS

Dear reader,

Thank you for reading *Whacked*. I hope you enjoyed it. If you did, please help others find it by sharing it with friends on social media and writing a review.

Sharing the book with your friends and leaving a review helps other readers decide to take the plunge into the nutty world of Lucie Rizzo. So please consider taking a moment to tell your friends how much you enjoyed the story. Even a few words expressing what you enjoyed most about the story is a huge help. Thank you!

Happy reading!
Adrienne

ACKNOWLEDGMENTS

Thank you to Josie and Fannie Palmer (a.k.a. The Ninja Bitches) for providing me with years of great material for my stories. Sadly, during the course of writing this book, both Josie and Fannie moved on to doggie heaven. Josie and Fannie were littermates and lived to be sixteen years old. Sixteen! My dear friends Kevin and Cindy lost their precious girls within three months of each other and, as all pet owners will understand, the loss was heartbreaking. Still, "the girls" provided a ton of love and laughter and I will always be grateful Cindy and Kevin allowed me to share them with my readers.

Thanks also to Tony Iacullo who continually provides me with legal angles I can use in my books. A big thank you to Scott Silverii who jokingly floated a title idea of Dog Collar Coitus and inadvertently gave me an idea for a dog who wound up saving a scene. Thanks also to Liliana Hart for the support and for sharing her knowledge. You guys are the best! To my editor, Gina Bernal, thank you for helping me transform my ideas into something I can be proud of.

Misty Evans, my writing partner and friend, thank you

for always answering those emergency emails when I've written myself into a corner and need help working my way out.

As usual, thank you to my guys for making me laugh every day. I love you.

Finally, thank you to my readers, who have embraced this series that I love so much.

ABOUT THE AUTHOR

Adrienne Giordano is a *USA Today* bestselling author of over twenty romantic suspense and mystery novels. She is a Jersey girl at heart, but now lives in the Midwest with her workaholic husband, sports-obsessed son and Buddy the Wheaten Terrorist (Terrier). She is a cofounder of Romance University blog and Lady Jane's Salon-Naperville, a reading series dedicated to romantic fiction.

For more information on Adrienne, including her Internet haunts, contest updates, and details on her upcoming novels, please visit her at:

www.AdrienneGiordano.com

agiordano@adriennegiordano.com

www.ingramcontent.com/pod-product-compliance
Lightning Source LLC
Chambersburg PA
CBHW071247190726

48292CB00007B/2440